For Daddy.

Some wounds never heal.

NE *by* BONE

tony johnston

a deborah brodie book
roaring brook press
new york

The author would like to thank the following people, whose guidance and support helped make this book possible: Susan Cohen; Bill Culver; Jed Joyce's grandmother; Ashley, Jennifer, Phyllis, Roger, and Dr. Samantha Johnston; Irene McDermott, Rex Mayreis and the San Marino Public Library staff; Gloria D. Miklowitz; Sue and Terry Minshull; Candace Moreno; Denise Nash; Roaring Brook Press; Sophie Skoda; Barbara Keesee Sparks; Betty Takeuchi; Vicky Taylor; Matthias Wehrle; and the writers known as the Lunch Bunch. Special thanks to Karen Hesse for her generous spirit. To Barry Moser, who read with care and enhanced the story with extraordinary grace and generosity, who shared the memory of his childhood friend, Nigger Tommy, so named to distinguish him from Barry's brother Tommy, I am most beholden.

Text copyright © 2007 by the Johnston Family Trust

A Deborah Brodie Book
Published by Roaring Brook Press
Roaring Brook Press is a division of Holtzbrinck Publishing Holdings Limited Partnership
143 West Street, New Milford, Connecticut 06776
www.roaringbrookpress.com

Library of Congress Cataloging-in-Publication Data
Johnston, Tony
 Bone by bone by bone / Tony Johnston. — 1st ed.
  p.   cm.
"Deborah Brodie book."
Summary: In 1950s Tennessee, ten-year-old David's racist father refuses to let him associate with his best friend Malcolm, an African American boy.
ISBN-13: 978-1-59643-113-3
ISBN-10:1-59643-113-X
[1. Racism—Fiction. 2. Race relations—Fiction. 3. Best friends—Fiction.
4. Friendship—Fiction. 5. Fathers and sons—Fiction.
6. Tennessee—History—20th century—Fiction.] I. Title.
PZ7.J6478Bne 2007
[Fic]—22   2006032923

10 9 8 7 6 5 4 3 2 1

Roaring Brook Press books are available for special promotions and premiums. For details, contact: Director of Special Markets, Holtzbrinck Publishers.

Book design by Míkael Vilhjálmsson
Printed in the United States of America
First edition August 2007

The time that this story takes place was more innocent and slower than now. Where I grew up, neighbor knew neighbor and stopped to speak; people left their doors unlocked; children made up games and played ditch 'em or baseball at twilight in the street till they were called home for supper.

But those were also mean days, when black people had to fight to gain an equal chance at life. Back then, especially in the South, they had to sit at the back of the bus; they could not use white bathrooms or drinking fountains or benches or hospitals or libraries or churches—or even look at a white person sideways—without dread of being lynched; black children were cheated out of a good education, for they could not attend the same schools as whites. Many were murdered for nothing in particular other than the color of their skin. They were killed by those trying to keep them from having what should have been theirs all along.

I was a child of those innocent-mean times. When I was thirteen and started high school, my father told me, "You ever bring a nigger home, I'll shoot him." I knew he meant business. He kept guns, to shoot cats that mated under our house. And once he shot at a man he thought to be a burglar in flight.

Though some people may be offended by it, I do not apologize for the raw language used in this book. It is my father's language and reflects a way of thinking that has troubled me my whole life.

In *A River Runs Through It*, Norman Maclean wrote that he was "haunted by waters." I am haunted by my father.

—T. J.

Last night I dreamed again that I had died.
For that dread hallucination keeps returning.
I am standing on the porch of the old house.
Frantically pummeling the screen door and screaming,
"He saw me! He's after me! Lemme in!"
A man opens the door. In slow motion
he brings up his shotgun, takes aim for my heart, fires.
The man is my daddy. And I am dead.

I.

The ghost possessed the liveliest eyes I had ever seen. They gleamed through the cutouts of the grimy sheet he was wearing like sparkly black diamonds.

I knew he was a ghost because it was Halloween. I knew he was a boy from his voice.

The boy was in trouble. Hell-with-Feathers (Hell for short), the world's meanest rooster, was attacking him without mercy. Hell had already caused him to spill the few sweets he had collected in a small, sorry sack. Now the old demon drubbed the sheet with pecks like the strikes of a spike, squawking all the while. And all the while the boy squalled, nearly pulling down the evening sky. He sounded little and scared.

"Git!" I hollered. "You just git!" I flapped my arms at Hell. He lunged and took after me. I picked up a stick and chased him through Harold Jasper's picket fence. From there Hell glared out, squawking murder.

In no time the boy recovered himself.

"One day I'm gonna eat you, squawk an' all!" he told the rooster.

He reminded me of Brer Rabbit, my favorite story-book character, full of spunk and sass. For the most part,

Brer Rabbit could outwit animals like Brer Fox, whose only thought was to grab him for supper. In this case, I speculated, the Brer Rabbit boy needed outside help, on account of being snarled up in that sheet.

"Hey," I said. "I'm David Church. Who're you?"

"Malcolm Deeter," the boy said. "You saved my life. I'll be your friend."

The whole time he spoke, he tried to wriggle free of his costume. Before he could do that, my daddy strode up. He and I were on our way home to get me set to go trickin' and treatin'. He'd lagged behind to visit with Jude Haggard, owner of Haggard's Drugstore, the only one in our town. Time to time my daddy had dealings with Jude on account of my daddy being a doctor.

"I am a modern-day Aesculapius," he often said in a jovial way. Aesculapius was the Greek god of medicine. He'd told me that umpteen-ump times. Daddy wanted me to become a doctor, too, "a chip off the old block." I could hardly wait to have my own doctoring bag. To spread open its dark mouth and fish out all the doctor paraphernalia—stethoscope of course, thermometer, rubber-tip hammer, pinpoint-sharp scissors, little brown bottles of Mercurochrome and iodine, syringes and all manner of ointments and plasters, and bundles of cherry-flavored suckers for the little ones. I could hardly wait to slip out like a bat on mysterious nighttime missions of mercy. Like Daddy.

My daddy was Franklin Church. He was extremely old. Forty-two years old in that year of 1951. He was of medium height and build, with large, blunt hands. His nails were flat, as though he'd let a hammer slip on each one. Ten whams total. His hair was a color called ginger, his eyes a blue that seemed to have been thinned with milk. Folks said I was his spitting image.

Daddy was dressed as immaculately as ever. Starched white shirt, stiff as rigor mortis. Dark pants, creased to the sharpness of a knife blade. Brown fedora. Bow tie, red as a rooster's comb. In my way of dress I didn't even slightly resemble him. In my untucked plaid shirt, baseball cap, and rumpled short pants, I looked like I'd been shot out of a cannon.

My daddy had a temper on him. Minute to minute you never knew which Daddy would be standing in his skin—good-humored, mean, or somewhere in between. The slightest thing could provoke him. You had to be careful how you talked to him; his hands were quick.

Right then I had the edgy feeling he was gonna blow. Sure enough, he commenced hollering, snatching at Malcolm's sheet. "Jesus Christ, boy! You can't wear that!"

I gasped. He did not understand the situation.

"Malcolm's a ghost," I said. "For Halloween."

"Take that damn thing off." Daddy's voice was flint.

"Y-yessir."

Malcolm removed it slowly, like it was his very skin. The sheet sloughed to the street. He stood there, a very little boy and skinny as a rake. His eyes were wide with fear.

Daddy pitched the sheet into a trash receptacle.

"Leave it be, hear?"

"Mama'll wear me out." Malcolm was nearly dissolved.

"You shoulda thought of that."

I hoped his mama would swoop down like a miracle and take care of him. But she didn't. She'd probably ducked into a nearby store to visit with an acquaintance.

I couldn't understand what was happening. I felt flushed, embarrassed.

"My daddy doesn't—"

"Hush up!"

Before I could explain, Daddy grabbed my hand and hustled me toward home. I looked back at Malcolm. Eight years old, I reckoned. And forlorn. My mind spun. The one thing I clung to was his Brer Rabbit-ness. I told myself, I bet that little ol' boy'll hang around and recover that sheet. I just bet he will.

"He's littler than me, Daddy," was all I could think of to say.

"He can't wear a sheet."

Mystified, I gulped and swung the talk to something else.

"He seems to be a nice boy," I half whispered. "I'd like him for my friend."

"He can't be your friend." His voice was so hard I flinched, expecting him to strike me.

"Why not, Daddy? He's nearly my same age. And he's full o' jingle."

"He's a nigger."

We walked on, neither speaking. Evening was deepening. The moon was on the rise. Stars clustered in the limbs of the walnut trees. I loved the *hush* of wind in the leaves, the scuffle of walnut husks under my feet.

I was familiar with each house we passed. Each was a friend I had known my whole life. Each had its own kindly face. I had known Daddy my whole life. I thought his face kindly at times. But with Malcolm it had been the face of a stranger.

Daddy had a way about him. When he wanted something, his voice turned to butter. Then he could coax radishes to becoming roses on their way up through the soil. He used that tone now.

"You're awful quiet," he said.

"Yessir."

"Something wrong?"

"I don't feel good."

He crouched and peered into my face.

"You hurt here?" he asked, poking my midsection gently for signs of bellyache.

"No sir."

"Here?" He checked my brow for fever.

"No sir."

"Where, then?" His tone turned sharp.

I couldn't tell him that my heart hurt.

"Shoot, David, ain't nothing wrong with you that a little trickin' and treatin' won't cure. Slip your costume on. You'll bounce right back to your own self again. I guarantee it." Like a slick snake-oil vendor, he shot me his flashiest grin.

The entire month of October, I'd thought of nothing else but Halloween. Halloween made me wild. Sometimes I got too excited to eat, just thinking about being allowed to stay out late. The dark hid the familiar. Replaced lampposts, houses, trees with hulking and fearsome things. Waiting.

Halloween, the dark grew deeper. I grew fearful and eager. I imagined the spookiness of Cherokee Street, where we lived, wrapped in the jack-o'-lantern gloom of that night, and the bounty of treats I'd get. Like a Milky Way bar or two, if I was lucky. I enjoyed breaking them apart, stretching the caramel out slowly, farther, farther, farther, till it became two separate pieces, each with a tiny thread at the end like a sweet wisp of cobweb. Boy, did I love Milky Ways.

❖　❖　❖

Our household would have been weighted toward women, but my mama died at my birth. I had only one picture to know her face. Grandmother Church, my daddy's mother, lived with us. And Old Ma, her mother, close on to a hundred years old. She was so enfeebled, she was stuck upstairs abed. Everybody said when I was real little, I'd misheard her name and called her Gold Ma. From then on she was Gold Ma to everybody.

Though she didn't much love sewing, Grandmother Church worked me up a Halloween costume. She was pretty good at it, having learned early on from Gold Ma.

That year, I recall, my heart's desire was to be a hobgoblin. The notion had come to me from a snatch of conversation I'd heard someplace. But nobody in our family had any idea just how such a creature might look.

"Sounds nasty to me," said Grandmother Church. "I'm not certain . . ." She looked anxious, as if even a costume of the thing could jump up and throttle her.

"You may be one hell of a seamstress, Mama, but even you can't create a costume that'll bite," said my daddy. "Go on, conjure one."

My grandmother mumbled, "Don't curse, Franklin."

As we entered the house that Halloween, my daddy roared with mirth, "Mama, where's that hobgoblin suit? This boy needs it to perk him up."

In no time I was in it.

"Well now," he said, giving me a little turn, "I believe we have here the hoblinest goblin in the whole damn state of Tennessee."

"Franklin, I wish you wouldn't curse," said Grandmother Church. She spoke as if each word cost her.

He turned to her, peeling off his charm. "If wishes were horses, beggars would ride," Daddy said.

After supper, Daddy and I went out into the night. Shoot, I was nine. I wanted to go alone. But, as usual, my grandmother insisted Daddy go, too. She was certain that hooligans would take advantage of the dark to murder, or at the very least, maim me.

That hour of the evening the air was chill, with an autumn tang. Dead old leaves went scraping their way down the street, whispering dead old secrets. Straggles of other trick-or-treaters giggled themselves along. Some had bars of soap to goop up windows where nobody was at home. I'd have loved to soap windows, but Daddy'd have blistered me good.

The moon was up. Silent and huge and gleaming. The color of a persimmon. For a long time I looked at it hovering over our town.

My breath held itself.

"What is it?" Daddy asked.

"The moon."

I wondered if Malcolm Deeter was out, too, with *his* daddy, under the enormous globe of light. Sure he was. He had vinegar. Right now he was probably floating up to somebody's door, trailing that ratty-tat sheet he'd fetched back, moaning *Booooo!* The thought made me feel a little better about his encounter with my daddy.

Seemed funny. What was so criminal about wearing a sheet? Wasn't as if Malcolm'd stuck up the Piggly Wiggly.

By then my sweets sack, a pillowcase, was pretty heavy. I hefted it now and then, trying to guess just how many Milky Ways were in my loot. There were plenty of houses to come. So we walked on, Daddy and I, clear through Halloween, wrapped in the haunted silence of the moon.

2.

It was friendship at first sight. From the time I met Malcolm Deeter, my other friends took a backseat. I'd see them, of course, but Malcolm, he was my heart-friend.

Malcolm and I could no more be separated than green from grass. My daddy had forbidden me to play with him, on account of his being colored. Though little by little I came to understand the barriers between Negroes and white folks, back then I knew of no rule about two boys not being friends. I convinced myself that Daddy'd been in a deep state of derangement when he'd lashed out at Malcolm. He'd gone crazy from the stare of the Halloween moon.

So, despite his warning, we played together. I didn't give a hoot about doing it, so long as I didn't get caught. Daddy'd probably thrash me with his leather bootlaces. Stung like the devil, but I'd lived through it before. Sometimes I worried that he might do something worse. But till he finally did, I had no idea how hateful a punishment could be.

I remember that summer. Our town was melting in the heat. "Hotter than three fat boys," according to my daddy.

Heat shimmered on the roads. Heat shimmered in the grass. Heat shimmered off the leaves of the magnolias. People moved more slowly and spoke more slowly than usual, doing their utmost to keep from turning to puddles. It was so hot, the tar on Cherokee Street softened up and got gummy. It smelled like the world before history, full of oozy pits that sucked big old animals in.

One early morning I heard something. *Thunk. Thunk. Thunk.* June bugs thumping my window screen? Nope. Too many thumps for bugs. Malcolm, flinging gravel. I groaned and got up.

"Hey, David," he said soon as I was outside, "wanna go to Jesus Pond?" That Malcolm was a firecracker, always popping with plans.

"Hush up or we'll get caught sure!" I whispered.

"We can play somethin'," Malcolm whisper-yelled, "in the cool. Come on!"

"Hush up, fool!"

Our household was still asleep. I ran back to the kitchen and grabbed us two doughnuts apiece. Then Malcolm and I sneaked off to Jesus Pond, named on account of the water striders that easily skimmed the surface, like Jesus.

It was cooler there than in town, though not much. We dabbled in the coffee-colored water, one eye out for cottonmouths, pretending we were ducks. Then we flopped on the bank, watching thin blue snake doctors zing themselves through the air. Gnats buzzed in our ears. Our T-shirts were plastered to us in wrinkles, like the damp skins of frogs. I felt sticky-hot all over, as if I'd been dipped in warm honey.

"David," said Malcolm, his voice jumping a notch.

"What?"

"Let's have us a pissin' contest."

I grinned. "I can out-piss you clear to Chattanooga."

Zzzzzt. Zzzzzt. Zippers slid down. Two yellow splurts of water arced over the pond and made a sizzling sound when they hit. We squirted ourselves dry, happy as two pups in a fire-hydrant factory. I gave it my damnedest, but Malcolm won.

"Now what?"

Malcolm looked around, his black eyes perking with inspiration. "Wanna play Brer Rabbit?"

That was our favored game, even though we were kind of old for it. From an early age, my daddy had read me stories about that long-eared bamboozler, who mostly bamboozled ol' Brer Fox.

"Ugh."

"What's that mean?"

"Means I cain't move," I told him.

"Don't be a ol' toad poop."

"I'm no stinkin' toad poop, but anyways, we got no tar for the Tar Baby."

Malcolm's eyes glittered over the scenery. "Nope," he said. "But we got mud. *Cool* mud." Once he fixed on an idea, there was no holding him. "You be Brer Fox an' I'll be Brer Rabbit."

"You're always Brer Rabbit," I complained.

"Okay, you be him. Now let's make us a Mud Baby."

Since he gave in without a fuss, I knew he was excited about it.

Malcolm and I took real care fashioning our Mud Baby. We were both barefoot. We squooshed close to the edge of the steamy pond, delighting in the loud slurps the mud made. Black muck oozed in a thick paste between our toes and soon covered our feet. We knelt down and clawed at it, like two big ol' cooters scooping out their nests.

Then we lugged armfuls of clay a short ways away, heaped it up and patted it to dark perfection. When our Mud Baby was done, we leaned against a cottonwood and considered him.

"Somethin's missing," Malcolm said.

I plopped my baseball cap on the Mud Baby's head. "There."

"Somethin's still missing."

Malcolm studied on it a long time. At last he took a stick and poked in a belly button. He smoothed it with a finger. "There."

"Reckon that's how God made people?" I asked.

"Prob'ly," said Malcolm. "But I wonder how He got the light inside."

"You mean the life?"

"I mean the light."

Ever after I wondered about that.

Malcolm knew the Tar Baby story by heart. He'd heard it about ten trillion times from his grandmother. He delighted in the impossible words, wrapping his tongue around each one.

The whole time he was spilling it out, Brer Fox— Malcolm—acted it out, too. With considerable huff-and-puff, he struggled with the Mud Baby and plopped it down in our "big road." Then he lay low in the reeds, just bustin' to see what Brer Rabbit—me—would do when that baby got uppity and refused to say howdy.

I threatened to "bust 'er wide open" and ended up with all fours gummed. Of course, I "butt 'er cranksided" and my head got stuck, too.

Malcolm and I, we hooted so hard we cried.

The world was someplace else. We were there. Beside the bank of a pond named Jesus. Gooped with mud. Talking, laughing, talking some more. Two boys in Tennessee, in summer.

❖   ❖   ❖

Our game was over. Malcolm and I were caked with nearly all the mud of Jesus Pond. Only our closest kin could possibly recognize us. We looked at each other and busted up again.

Came a sudden crashing in the cattails.

"Duck!" I hissed.

Malcolm must have seen the man, too. He didn't need to be told twice to take cover.

Slur Tucker came reeling along with his fishing gear. And a gutting knife. He was bald-headed, with small, wide-apart eyes, so he looked like an evil and monster potato bug from where we were crouched in concealment. Slur was always so lit with liquor, his words had to lean on each other. That's how come he got his name. He was a devil, all right. The kind who'd stomp your guts out for fun—especially if you were a Negro. Even a glance from him could harm a person, maybe sear the flesh on his very bones. I believed that and looked past him.

Malcolm and I hunkered down, motionless, till we became one with the muck. We stayed put till Slur staggered on to wherever his feet were going.

It was about two o'clock when I traipsed into the house. Grandmother Church was sweeping the porch. Seemed she was always sweeping, as if it were the one thing she could do to keep the world organized.

Grandmother Church was tall and thin, with skin so light she looked liked she'd been dipped in flour. She always wore grim little glasses. And the same pair of earrings, big and black, like overgrown gumdrops. Her hair was a natural snow-white. But somebody'd told her blue-haired ladies know everything. So once a week, faithful as Friday, she applied a product called Henna from Heaven. When it was dried and combed out and the sun backlit it, her hair encircled her head in a soft blue shimmer.

My grandmother was a timid woman, flinchy, I guess you'd say. About as far from Gold Ma as you could get. She was fearful of everything that walked—and a sight of things that didn't.

Robbers were her chief concern. Though she carried her pocketbook "clutched close to her breast like a suckling babe," Daddy said, whenever she ventured out, she always anchored her paper money to the inside of her brassiere with a big ol' safety pin. Nights, she propped a slat-back chair under her doorknob to keep burglars at bay.

When she wasn't sweeping or keeping house, she was reading. My grandmother loved books. She read mostly to herself, but she read the Bible to me. The Bible was the one book you better know cover to cover, if you were to be saved. Grandmother never told me saved from what.

She spoke so little, Daddy called her "taciturn as a churn." Sometimes she was so quiet, I thought maybe she didn't like me. I learned that her silence came from an accumulation of travail, built up like bark on a tree. But that was later on.

When she caught sight of me, crusted with mud and what all, Grandmother Church *did* say something: "David, don't you set foot on my Persian."

I snorted, imagining myself treading on some person from a foreign land. Only she was speaking of her carpet. It was old. It was revered. I was young. I was not revered, particularly not in my muddy state.

Because of his doctoring, my daddy kept few regular hours. And now, unfortunately for me, he was home.

"Mama, I'll handle this," he said, peering over the front page of the *News Free-Press*. "Well, well, what do we have here?" His voice was edged with ice.

"B-Brer Rabbit, sir."

"You mean *Mud* Rabbit?"

"Yessir."

"You been playing alone?"

"No sir."

"Who you been playing with?" he asked, though I was certain he already knew. Malcolm and I'd been sneaking around for some time. And Daddy was no dummy.

"Malcolm," I mumbled, as if I were confessing to murder.

"Speak up, David."

"With Malcolm Deeter."

"You're forbidden to play with that little jigaboo."

I felt a stab of cold in my belly.

"He's my friend," I whispered.

"You deaf, boy? I told you long ago, there'd be no fraternizing with niggers." He grabbed me by one ear and shouted into the other. "Understand me?"

"Yessir."

"This damn fool escapade's going to cost you dearly."

My grandmother watched, knuckles to her teeth, but didn't make a peep. She never took my part in anything. I didn't know why, and it enraged me, how she always went along with Daddy.

Finally he released me. My ear burned and I kept rubbing at it. He stared at me till I wanted to run. Fear crawled up my collar. I waited for him to fetch his bootlaces. I decided when he whipped me, I'd show him. I wouldn't cry. But he didn't make a move for the laces. His eyes just kept glittering at me.

"Seems keeping you and Malcolm apart is like trying to stop a train with chewing gum. Well, in this house *I'm* kingpin. So, I'm laying down my Nigger Rule."

Grandmother Church's skirt rustled as she started to leave the room.

"Stay right there, Mama. I want you to hear this." Daddy turned back to me. "David, you'll go round me no matter what, so play like hell—*outside*. But he can never set foot in this house. Rule's real simple: you ever let that nigger in, by God, I'll shoot him."

He formed his words with such a calm, I knew he'd planned this, cold as ice. And I had no doubt whatever he'd do just what he said. Though I tried hard not to, I began to cry. I couldn't stop.

Daddy didn't seem to notice.

When I told Malcolm about it, he stared at me for a long time. Then he said, "My daddy. He'd never do me like that. Yo' daddy. He's a devil."

white people in our town employed Negroes in ay or another. To cook or do heavy work or any tment of odd jobs. Through the back door. That's where they entered. But Daddy did not permit coloreds in our house anytime. That puzzled me, because I'd heard snatches about somebody close to him, way, way back, a Negro woman who slid through my mind sometimes, like a phantom.

Anyhow, Negroes simply could not come in. But never before had Daddy threatened to shoot one.

Because of Daddy's obsession, a white woman named Lily did for my grandmother. Lily came on Mondays and holidays to do the ironing. She also entered through the back.

Since we had no regular help, I'd learned to cook. And I was good at it. My favorite chore was fixing the biscuits. I loved to measure the dry ingredients in the hollow of my hand, like my grandmother did, scooping the sugar and flour from the cool metal innards of the possum-belly table in our kitchen. I loved to sneak sips of buttermilk when nobody was looking. To fold and roll the dough and cut it out with a jelly glass into small, soft moons.

That evening I'd worked up some biscuits on my own.

"Call your daddy to supper, David," said my grandmother.

"Yes'm." I called from the bottom of the stairs, not to rile him.

Daddy came directly.

"Well now, doesn't this look tasty," he said, sitting down at the table. Fried chicken with milk gravy, snap beans with fatbacks, mashed potatoes and my puffy biscuits steamed up before us.

My daddy bowed his head. We all did, like heavy-headed flowers in a garden. "Lord, we are thankful for this food," Daddy said. "And for this fine family. And for the fine boy who prepared these delectable biscuits."

He helped himself to the chicken neck, which he considered the choicest part. "Here, David," he teased, passing me the platter, "I saved you the Pope's nose." He also called this piece of the bird "the part that went over the fence last."

I was about to say something I'd regret, when the telephone rang. My daddy pushed back his chair and, mopping chicken grease from his face, answered it.

"Going out, Mama," he suddenly announced. "I'll be back."

"What about supper?"

My belly knotted, and I waited for him to snarl something like, "You checking up on me?" Instead he said, "I'll have some later on. Cold biscuits and buttermilk. Can't beat that."

Right off I noticed his doctoring valise in the chair beside the sofa. "Hey, Daddy left this," I said, swinging the bag in my grandmother's face. "I'll catch up to him." I tagged along with him whenever I could, to build on my doctoring know-how.

"No, David."

My grandmother looked grim. She'd gone to some trouble to prepare the food Daddy'd abandoned. On account of the Nigger Rule, I didn't feel hungry. But to please my grandmother, I nibbled at a chicken wing. I spread butter and jelly on a biscuit, broke it into bits, and poked them around my plate. I hoped she wouldn't notice I wasn't really eating.

Soon as I dared, I said, "I'll take something up to Gold Ma."

"Thank you, David."

I looked out my window. Over our town. Down Cherokee Street. The streetlamps were on. Their dim light spilled where their necks, like metal swans', curved down. I savored the first night sounds. The creak of crickets hidden in the grass. A Victrola playing heartbreak notes. The purr of cars returning to garages like great metal homing pigeons. The stutter of a Rain Bird. The lonely songs of cats.

But cats weren't the real thing on my mind. The real thing was Malcolm. Why shouldn't he come into our home? Other Negroes couldn't. But Malcolm was different. Malcolm was my friend. Friends should be allowed in. Right then I set myself a goal: to get Daddy to change the Nigger Rule.

3.

In our town—maybe in the whole of the South—there's an idea floating like dandelion fluff through the air: when a boy turns ten, he's nearly a man.

One day, with the first ray of sun, I took two stairs at a time, waking the dead as I stomped my way down. "I'm ten! I'm ten!" I hooted like a loon.

"Well, you act about seven," Daddy said, smiling. He was already in the kitchen. He looked me over, then said, "Here, let's get us your measurement."

The frame of the back door was for measuring the height of family members. If you looked carefully, there were lots of squiggly pencil marks—some faint, some dark—that to outsiders might look like secret code. They recorded where the top of somebody's head had reached on a certain date. Those dates leaned back and back, way into the 1800s. Nobody since had dared paint over those marks. Anytime I wanted, I could see how my grandmother and Daddy and Uncle Lucas, his brother, had all grown up, taller, taller, taller, like plants reaching for sun.

Though I had no memory of him, there was a mark to show my granddaddy's height, a little slash that on sight made him real. And I could even see Gold Ma's growth! "She's a ol' marker fossil," Uncle Lucas had said once.

Gold Ma's people had notched their heights with knives, as if not taking chances with Time. Alongside one little gash, the doorjamb read, *Carolina, 3 ft., 1 in., 1859.* Close by, but higher, were lines representing her brothers: Utah, Texas, Kansas, Colorado, Montana, Dakota, Missouri, Oklahoma, New Mexico, Oregon, Nevada, Kentucky, Washington, Florida, California, and Tennessee, of course. They'd planned on a passel of children, so the parents named them for states. That was the lore in our house. It was a heavy thing to imagine that Gold Ma had stood next to this frame, just like me, to think that she'd once had a name—that she'd been young.

I reached up and touched that old board.

"Come on, David," Daddy said, "stand up tall."

And I did. I stretched as much as I could, to seem big.

"Keep your feet flat. Don't cheat."

So I flattened my feet—sort of. I bet Daddy'd cheated. I bet they all had, especially Lucas and Gold Ma, when it was their turn to be measured.

"Four feet, nine inches!" Daddy bellowed proudly, like old Noah measuring the ark. "Just like a sunflower, Mama! He's sprouting tall as a damn sunflower!" He marked my height on the frame—dark and deep.

My grandmother let the curse go, probably because

it was my birthday. Instead, she said, "Breakfast's ready."
Ordinarily, I'd have been wolfing down hotcakes fast as
she could slide 'em from the griddle. Not now.

"Can't I open my presents first?"

"Breakfast will get cold," said Grandmother Church.

"Daddy," I moaned like a dying calf.

"Mama, the boy's about to pop. Cover those hotcakes
with a plate. They'll keep."

So my grandmother brought out the presents. There
were two: one long and narrow, one big and flat. That was
the one I fixed on. I grabbed for the big box.

"Hold on, David," my daddy said. He handed me the
skinny one, wrapped in blue tissue paper. I took it and
shook it close to my ear. Something heavy slung around
inside there.

"Can you guess?" Daddy asked, leaning toward me
eagerly.

"Nope." I was poppin' to open the other one.

"Go on, try."

I groaned and shook it again. "Paperweight?"

Daddy's eyes rolled. "You can use a brick to weight
paper. You think I'd *invest* in one?" My mind gyrated all
over the place and ended up on a thing closer to home.
"Bone!" I said triumphantly.

"Yes, David, a bone," my daddy said with scorn. "We'll
cook us some soup soon as you open it up."

I thought it was a pretty good guess, what with my doctoring goal. Finally, I gave up and just dove in. It was a bowie knife, sharp as the devil, with my initials, *D.C.C.*, on the leather sheath. Daddy's idea of what a ten-year-old boy needed.

"Well? Don't you just love it?"

I waited. Then I lied, "I love it."

I snapped up the other present and tore into it. I wasn't going to piddle around guessing. I already knew what was inside, I just *knew* it—a pair of long pants, the difference between a baby and a grown-up. I'd have bet my bottom dollar on it.

Only it wasn't long pants. It was a raincoat.

I gave out a little bleat. Then I flung the raincoat to the floor, like it was some kind of snake.

"Damn it!" The words spurted out. *"I hate it!"*

The room went quiet. Daddy looked at me. "Well now," he said. I waited for him to wring my neck.

But no. Like always, Daddy surprised me—now, with a strange softness, as if remembering that he was a boy once. He didn't lift a hand to me.

"We'll be back, Mama." Without another word, Daddy folded the raincoat carefully and put it in the box. He drove me downtown. To the dry-goods store. Even though it was early, he got the owner, Mr. Pruett, to open up. "Somebody bought this damn raincoat in their sleep,"

Daddy explained, holding it out. And I knew he felt bad about it. In a blink he exchanged it, and he bought me a pair of long pants.

"There now, David, honey," Daddy said to me, placing a hand on my shoulder. "Now you've got your heart's desire."

4.

While I was growing up, upstairs Gold Ma was growing old. She had lived in this house, our house, since she was a little girl, a very long time ago. It was her house then. And her mama's. And her daddy's. Neither my grandmother nor my daddy nor I had yet been born.

Now Gold Ma lived in our old back bedroom, the place in the house most touched by sun. She lay in a high four-poster bed all day long. Her mind was sharp as a well-stropped razor, but her body, she mourned, "had treasoned" her. Weakened as she was by the weight of her years, she could no longer walk by herself. Unless she was in her wicker wheelchair, she did not get out of bed, except to use the toilet. She did that with help. Whenever she needed somebody to escort her, she'd ring a little bell on her bedside table. Then, one of us would go to her on the run.

Whenever I entered Gold Ma's room, the smell enfolded me like a crazy quilt. A mingling of wilting flowers and sweet talcum and false teeth and cold cream and bunion pads and VapoRub and cough syrup and fresh bedsheets and yarn and flannel gowns and Bible leather and Ipana tooth powder and witch hazel and papery skin and sour breath and mothballs and peppermints and pee.

It smelled of things that had happened long ago. And of something waiting to happen. The room was steeped in the smell of an old lady.

One day I heard the little bell ring. I was in a fret to leave and go find Malcolm, so I ignored it. I clopped like a bovine down the stairs and was nearly out the screen door when Grandmother Church stopped me in flight.

"Gold Ma's calling," she said.

I knew better than to groan, so I went up to Gold Ma's room.

"Hey," I said. I hoped her business would go fast. Malcolm and I had plans. We were going to pitch horseshoes till one of us won the Championship of the World.

Gold Ma was propped up on a triangular pillow, the bedclothes jumbled around her. Her hair flowed over the pillow like Rapunzel's, only hers was white, not gold. She was swathed in her favorite kimono, a gift from my uncle Lucas.

Uncle Lucas, loud as a bass drum. And funny. And true. Said whatever spanged into his head. His best friend, Junior Junior Davis, once told me with pride, "Yore uncle, he's jest wile as a acre o' snakes." Wild maybe, but I loved him. I wished he'd come visit more. I could talk to him. Just like I could talk to Malcolm. Just like Malcolm, Uncle Lucas had a headful of bright ideas like a big bowl of shiny jellybeans. He'd know how to break the Nigger Rule—without getting anybody killed.

Gold Ma's kimono was black and yellow, the colors of a wasp. The long sleeves swam at her wrists, making her hands seem tiny as a baby doll's. The smoothness of the silk made her skin look crinklier than it actually was.

Gold Ma squinted. "David," she said, her eyes tiny and bright as a chicken's.

"Yes'm."

"What do you want?"

"I heard the bell. You need to use the toilet?"

"Don't pry," shot Gold Ma. "Prying's impolite."

Though her body was wizened up like a raisin, her tongue was sharp as a boning knife.

"I'm not pryin'. I just thought—"

"Stop your thinking. Help me up." Then she grumbled, "Damn. I'd rather use the privy."

In the backyard we had a privy, which Daddy called the Last Ring of Hell, it smelled so nasty. To my grandmother, it was the Outdoor Convenience. It was nearly tumbled down with years and draped in honeysuckle vines. The honeysuckle fumes were so heavy and sweet, they masked the reek till you got up close. So many Churches had made use of the place, their backsides had polished the wooden seat like glass.

A rusted ax leaned against one side of the little ruin. I never was sure why. Maybe in case somebody got the notion to chop the whole thing down.

Though our house'd had indoor plumbing as of 1909, Grandmother Church insisted in her timid way on going outside. Times change; my grandmother did not. And so, whenever Nature called at nighttime, my daddy or I would escort her (and Gold Ma till she slowed down at ninety) to the reeking old privy.

One time, at full moon, while my grandmother was doing her business, a big ol' rat jumped into her lap. Instantly, the door burst open. Out shot the rat. Out shot my grandmother, gone wild as a berserker.

"Attacked by vermin! Attacked by vermin!" she commenced to holler at the top of her lungs, sprinting for the house, whupping her arms like a turkey in full flap, stumbling over weeds and hummocks, hobbled by her own drawers, which were, sworn to by my daddy, who'd witnessed the whole scene, "still at half-mast."

Grandmother Church moved so quick, Daddy had a hard time catching up to her. Even then he couldn't speak. He could only sputter. He was laughing so, he nearly ruptured. When he finally got ahold of himself, Daddy asked her in a voice full of deviltry, "Why didn'tcha wait for me, Mama?" He told everybody he knew—and plenty of perfect strangers—about "the vermin incident." My grandmother was so mortified, for a month, every time she saw Daddy, she dissolved.

She kept on using the privy. But she took to lugging a

skillet with her, to cover her lap—and to swing at varmints.

This day, I helped Gold Ma out of bed, slow, slow. She inched to the edge, then slid down with great care, till her feet touched the planks of the wooden floor.

"Damned if the North Pole hasn't invaded," she said. "At one time, this was Tennessee."

"Yes'm." I always agreed with her because Gold Ma was a whole lot touchier than Daddy.

"How're my azaleas doing?" she asked suddenly. Her azaleas were her pride.

They grew along the shaded side of our house, where they bloomed in clots of pink and purple and red. Once she'd spent long hours tending them, seeing that the soil was tilled, that they were free of bugs, that they had plenty of manure—"a shitload," Uncle Lucas said. People who passed by could not resist comment. They'd call out things like "Lovely azaleas, Carolina. You've sure enough got the touch." "Those blooms are real prizewinners." "I swan, you're a born gardener." That was before she'd become bedridden.

I supported Gold Ma's weight, which was not much more than a child's. "Your flowers are just fine," I said, trying to keep her shuffling toward the toilet. Malcolm was waiting to pitch horseshoes in the yard. I itched to get downstairs. Still, I moved slowly, I thought. But I must have hurried her.

"Slow down or you'll break my neck," she snapped. "I know what you're up to."

"I'm not up to anything, Gold Ma."

"You're lying. You're in a rush, so's you can play with that little nigra boy."

I didn't say a word, but inside I flared. She's an old lady, I told myself. She doesn't know what she's saying. But she did.

"Don't think just 'cause I'm old I've got no idea what's goin' on. Ya know, old's not the same as dead."

"Yes'm."

Gold Ma drowned me with her watery eyes.

"You keep clear o' him, David. Nigras aren't people."

I shot her a look laced with hatred.

Gold Ma leaned on me while I lifted the toilet lid. A frog was swimming inside.

Our house was old. The plumbing was bad. "Worse than Gold Ma's," Uncle Lucas liked to joke. Every now and then, by some small miracle, a frog would set off on an upstream journey and surface in one of the toilets. When that happened, Grandmother Church would call me to dispose of it.

"What's that, David, a turd?"

"It's a frog."

The old lady glared at it.

"Frogs are like nigras," she announced. "Dirty and swart and ugly as all hell. They're trying to take over. Get it out o' there—mash it."

Her words stuck me like a hat pin.

Hateful old hellion! I thought. The way she spread venom, I wondered why God hadn't already reared up and struck Gold Ma down.

Silence slipped into the room and saved us from hating each other.

I scooped the frog from the toilet bowl and set it on the windowsill. It squatted there, still as a rubber statue.

When she'd done her business, slow, slow, I helped Gold Ma back to bed.

"Read to me," she said, giving me a tight little smirk. I knew there would be no horseshoes that day.

"Can't I just tell—"

"You do like I say an' read." That sly, gloaty smile slid across Gold Ma's face again. Last Ring of Hell, I thought. Daddy's was the privy; Gold Ma was mine.

I read *Kidnapped*, heavy with Scottish dialect. It was over my head and I fumbled a lot. Gold Ma fussed a lot about my blunders. Reading that book was like stumbling over stream-drowned boulders.

The frog didn't stir the entire time. It was probably mortified at how badly I read. When I was done, I took it in my cupped hands. Then it wouldn't quit squirming. I walked downstairs and into the garden. I grinned and released the frog into Gold Ma's azaleas.

5.

On Sundays we always went to church. Our church was the Centenary Methodist Church. Though I asked a string of questions, I was never clear on what a Methodist was. Understanding was not in the bargain. Confused, I still went to church.

When I woke up, I could tell if it was Sunday. Sundays had a quiet to them. Like angel breath.

Our whole family attended church together—my daddy, my grandmother, Gold Ma, with the help of her wheelchair, and me. After a gorgeous breakfast of bacon and eggs, cinnamon rolls, and warm cornbread slathered with butter, we settled ourselves into my daddy's automobile. An antique Buick, long and black, with whitewall tires and a convertible top. Daddy was proud of that car—a sin, my grandmother informed him. He just let that comment roll, probably because it was Sunday.

On Sundays my daddy drove with a calm. That was the only time.

We wore our good clothes when we went to church. Everybody did. The children wore shoes. The women wore fancy dresses and hats with veils and white gloves. The men wore suits and ties.

People gathered at our church. Some people we hadn't seen all week. They were dressed up, too, the children in particular, as if at any time somebody might snap their picture. Sometimes a faithful dog went along and got into the picture with them.

People moved slowly. They spoke softly. Because it was Sunday.

Our church was not of much size. It was made of bricks, painted white. To me it looked like a great big dove perched upon the lawn. It had windows with stained-glass pictures made someplace up North.

When it was time for the service, we moved to the inside of the church, which was also white. Muttering like doves, we filled the wooden pews. The minister spoke about Jesus our Savior. About love thy neighbor. Then we opened our hymnals and sang, about how we were all God's children. We sang sweet and we sang loud, so that people already up in Glory would hear us. We sang so that God would know we loved Him.

I tried to sing sweet. I know I sang loud.

When the service was over, the Methodists wandered out into the yard. They lingered there, talking about nothing much. Talking softly because it was Sunday.

On Sundays Malcolm's family always went to church, too. He'd told me all about it. His church was the New Hope

Baptist Church. Like me and the Methodists, Malcolm was baffled about just what Baptists were. Like me, that didn't stand in the way of him having to go.

Malcolm's whole family attended church together— his mother, his father, his grandmother and grandfather, and his brothers and sisters. Malcolm had no Gold Ma. He had a great-granduncle, a little raisin of a man. They owned an old car, a beater, but his family preferred to walk from their house down to Ninth Street.

The Deeter family wore their good clothes when they went to church. The children wore shoes. The women wore fancy dresses and hats that had surely cost flocks of birds their lives and white gloves. The men wore suits and ties. The children wore their best finery, as if at any time somebody might snap their picture. Sometimes a faithful dog went along and got into the picture with them.

People gathered at the Baptist church. Some people, Malcolm said, the Deeters hadn't seen all week. They were gussied up, too. They moved slowly. They spoke softly. Because it was Sunday.

Malcolm's church was not of much size. It was made of slatted wood, painted white, a lot of it flaking off. He said he thought it looked like Noah's Ark, perched upon a mountaintop when the Flood had dried up. It had window panels of yellowy glass made in our town someplace.

When it was time for the service, Malcolm told me,

everybody moved to the inside of the church, which was also white. Muttering like doves, they filled the wooden benches. The preacher spoke about Jesus our Savior. About love thy neighbor. Malcolm said that they felt fire in their bones and—just like spontaneous fires—people burst into ringing songs. When they sang, they sang sweet and they sang loud, so that people already up in Glory would hear them. They sang so that God would know they loved Him.

Malcolm said he sang louder than anybody. I believed him.

6.

When I was born, so the story went, the day they brought me home, my daddy burst into the nursery bearing a full-blown skeleton. Human. The bones were yellowed. Like old teeth. And clacked against each other in a hollow song.

"David, honey," Daddy said in a crouch next to my crib, "meet Fats, your first playmate. You're gonna learn every one of his bones by heart. You, baby boy, gonna be a doctor."

My mama newly dead, that fatherly gesture must have cost him. But maybe Daddy didn't link them, Mama and the skeleton.

The story went, Daddy hung the bone man from my crib. Like a mobile. Eye level. So I could see those bones clearly. That was the beginning of my education.

To become a doctor you had to attend the right schools, my daddy said. There was one, the Barlow Academy, up North. New York, maybe.

It was far from us, but it was the right school to climb up the doctor ladder. Pupils entered Barlow at age thirteen—if they passed the entrance examination. On the day of my birth, Daddy wrote a letter to the headmaster of the Barlow Academy apprising him that the application for admission of David Chambers Church was imminent—in thirteen years.

Of course, it wasn't just bones Barlow focused on. Vocabulary and history and mathematics and geography would be a prime part of the test. But Daddy, he homed in on the human anatomy mostly.

Daddy labeled as many of Fats's bones as he could, with little rectangular name tags looped over the particular bone in question, then pulled right back on through the loop again. His theory was that the information Fats offered so freely—the fluttering name tags, the bones themselves—would, by merely being within my range of view, be absorbed into my tiny cranium.

When a bone was impossible to tag on account of its size or location or some other complication, Daddy illuminated it with a gummy paper dot, stuck right to the slick surface. This task accomplished, Fats looked like a skeletal dictionary. All businesslike and stickery.

When I got bigger, the name tags got switched for numbers. My daddy had me make up a list of the bones of the human skeleton—206 in all, each with its own number. (Drawing up that list was a study in itself, Daddy said.) I took it with me everyplace I went, to look over every chance I got.

Sometimes I imagine myself way back then, lying in

my crib, bald as a bulb, staring with my new eyes up at Fats, also bald as a bulb. Sometimes I wonder what I'd thought of him, so long and leering and lanky. Sometimes I wonder what he'd thought of me, so small and soft and sobby.

Instead of reading to me at bedtime (except for Brer Rabbit and certain other holy tomes), my daddy spoke the names of bones. My small ears heard his hymn: *sternum, scapula, fibula, tarsal, metatarsal.* Over and over and over again.

I began speaking young, beginning, of course, with squeaks and gurgles and grunts. Once, when I was maybe nine months old, Daddy was seated in my room when he heard an astonishing thing spurt from my lips—a word. He scooped me up, soiled diaper and all, set me on his lap in his Buick automobile, and drove downtown. He busted into his hangout, Russ Russell's barbershop.

"Listen."

The place fell silent. Everybody listened, intent.

"Ma-co-po."

Daddy translated. "Metatarsal."

My first word. So the story went.

7.

In our town, the birth of a boy was a very special miracle. Such an event required a special gift. Some boy babies received baseballs and baseball gloves. Gloves with a deep, rich aroma of leather, good for catching and for thumping with a fist. At first they were too big, of course.

Other boy babies, the real lucky ones, received guns. Those prized weapons were to be used on the very first day the little fellows made it off their knees and were able to totter upright. Those guns were too big for the babies, too, but *Lord*, they'd grow into them.

At birth, I myself, apart from Fats the skeleton man, was presented with a twelve-gauge shotgun. It was also given to me by my daddy.

There were guns in our house, a small arsenal, to cover a multitude of needs. To hunt bear, Daddy had a 30.06 rifle. To hunt deer, a 30.30. For coons, a .22. For dove, quail, and other game birds, a twenty-gauge.

All of those firearms rested in a rack made of polished walnut. It hung from the wall near the front of the house, between the parlor and the sitting room.

When he was not yanking tonsils out or setting bones, my daddy enjoyed hunting. I remember one time he went duck hunting with his friend Miraculous Call, named that on account of being born to a father over eighty years of age. Whenever his parentage came up, eyebrows were raised. People said, "Miraculous."

They set out early one morning in Miraculous's Ford car. Before they'd left, my daddy asked me to snap their picture with his Brownie camera. I still have that picture—a moment caught in black and white. It is daybreak. Two men stand beside a bulbous sedan, each with one foot on the running board, their arms draped over each other's shoulders. They are both cradling shotguns, broken at the breech. They are grinning.

That evening they returned jubilant, a string of dead ducks festooned across both sides of the car like limp bowling pins.

"There're fifty-seven, David!" Daddy hollered. "Count 'em!"

I didn't. And though I couldn't put it into words, I knew something had been lost that morning, along with all those ducks. The world felt colder. Fifty-seven. To this day, I hate that number.

Most people we knew didn't hunt cats. Daddy did. There were lots of strays in our neighborhood—gray, striped, marmalade, the tortoise variety—a real motley crew. I remember one old tom in particular. He was black and white, heavy in the shoulders, tapering toward the tail. There were notches in his ears, from battle. A sort of fur-covered football player. I named him Jim Thorpe, for a famous athlete.

These wanderers slipped through our days and nights. I enjoyed their soft comings and goings.

There was a little square opening on one side of our house. It was the mouth of a vent under the floorboards. Malcolm and I had crawled under there plenty of times. On our bellies, we'd scrunched ourselves along with our elbows, soldier-style, shuddering the whole time from the touch of the cobwebs that snagged at us like tickly spiders. When we were in position, we listened for voices inside the house. We longed to learn dark secrets.

Maybe my blue-haired grandmother had a blue-haired admirer—that was Malcolm's hope. I itched for hush-hush tidbits about Daddy's phantom, the mysterious colored woman I'd heard tell of now and then. Trouble was, the oak floorboards were thick as a fist, creating a slab of silence. Whatever secrets passed above us were muffled like the voices of spirits.

The cats knew about the vent, so some nights they made visitations to that hole. Then, gathered beneath the foundation of our house, they began "to woo their ladies," my daddy said.

Their caterwauling set him into an upswing. Whenever

he heard the first wails, he'd snatch the twenty-gauge from the rack.

"Hear that, David?" His voice got high, eager. "The sopranos are at it. Let's pepper the furry sons o' bitches."

Then we'd slip out the door and, like big-game hunters, we'd stalk those cats. The gun wasn't loaded with real shot. Not on cat nights. For felines, my daddy used rock salt. He emptied the shells, crammed them with salt, and crimped them up again. Rock salt didn't kill the cats, just encouraged them not to return.

"Stings like hell," Daddy said. "Makes 'em loop the air like circus artists."

Shooting cats made me squeamish. I was in no rush to join in.

One night the cats were singing. It was not long after my go-round with Gold Ma over Malcolm and the frog in her toilet. Though I was reluctant to, I followed Daddy. I knew I had no choice.

"Here, David," my daddy said in fine humor, "you do the honors." He shoved the gun into my hands.

Our intended victim must have heard us approach. He'd slunk from the cat hole and was now crouching right still alongside the house in the growing gloom. A small, mottled shape, no longer gargling his serenade. Jim Thorpe. Petrified. His eyes, like green purie marbles, gleamed straight through me. I felt sick at my stomach.

"I can't," I strangled out.

"Shoot," Daddy said.

I shook but could not speak.

"Shoot." His voice darkened.

Oh, God. The shotgun kicked into my shoulder, though I don't remember feeling it. I heard the blast, then a horrible screech. My belly flipped like Jim Thorpe. I dropped the gun and fled to my room. There I sat, feeling darker than the dark.

After what seemed a long while, my daddy came in. There was no sign of the shotgun. I was sitting on my bed, staring at nothing.

"Hey, sonny boy, why'd you run off?" he asked, jovial as could be. "It was just a cat."

I didn't answer.

"Cat got your tongue?" Daddy asked.

"I like cats," I whispered.

8.

A dark thing moved among us, known as the Ku
Klux Klan. Nobody much spoke of it outright, but ever
since I was little, I'd heard snatches about it. The group
liked to keep things pretty stirred up. There'd been a
number of killings hereabouts. Sometimes Daddy reported
to Grandmother Church from the *News Free-Press*: "Another
nigger dead near Hawk's Woods. A strangulation," he said.
"Work appears to be Klan."

I shuddered. To me, ducks and cats were a fearful loss,
but this was *people*.

I'd jigsawed together a picture of this group that
flared out in gangs, hunting folks. They were some kind
of knights, so they said. But they hid in sheets and hoods.
And by nightfall did frightful things.

Weren't knights heroes who performed great deeds?
Maybe Klan was a thing clear only to grown-ups. I was just
a boy. I didn't understand.

Once, I heard our phonograph mourn. Miss Billie Holiday
sang about Strange Fruit, the bodies of Negroes hanging,
swinging, burning, rotting from the branches of Southern
trees.

That night I dreamed of hooded figures swarming the ground. Swarming Malcolm's house. Phantoms cradling shotguns. They dragged him from his bed where he slept, out through the shadows, to the waiting trees.

"Malcolm! Break free! Run!" I screamed in the dark of my dream, shivering and sweating and gulping air.

Instantly, Daddy was there.

"What is it, David?"

I couldn't speak. I just shook.

"Here now. It's all right."

Daddy held me till the sun came up.

9.

Malcolm and I hardly talked about school, like it
was somehow off-limits. He went to his school, I went to
mine. And that was the name of that tune. We saw each
other when class was out and we had time to burn. We
could keep on playing because Malcolm hadn't told his
folks about the Nigger Rule. But when I think back on it,
maybe they didn't want him anywhere near me from the
beginning, on account of Daddy was Daddy.

Once, when I was maybe eleven, Malcolm and I discovered a cave, an event that caused all other thoughts to fade
in my mind. It was fall. Live oaks clustered in that place,
shouldering each other for sun, their boles big around as
behemoth legs. Withered leaves cascaded from the oaks
near the cave's damp mouth, turning the ground to rust.

We biked down there—at least I did. On my royal blue
Schwinn. I'd attached playing cards to the spokes of the
wheels with clothespins to make a fine racket. Malcolm
didn't have a bike, so he walked and I pedaled alongside
him, slow as I could without toppling.

Later on, we learned that our secret place was Black
Bob Cave, and it had at one time served as a hideout for
Confederate troops. The cave's tunnels spread like the

veins of a hand, back into the depths of the earth. Generations of boys had known it. Now it was our turn.

Black Bob Cave was deliriously dank and dark, but for the dim light leaking in at the mouth. It was odorous with earth and mold and bat guano and mice and pee. It was rank with possibilities.

One day we were rooting around in the cave, sweeping flashlights over the place, and came upon an old rag. Malcolm found it. Dug it outta the ground with a branch. Except it wasn't a rag at all. It was a hood, rotting and nearly eaten through. I stared at the ragged eye cutouts. Though they were empty as dead sockets, they still held plenty of hate. I imagined a face inside it, breathing softly, sucking the cloth in, out. Malcolm dropped the thing like a venomous snake. So, then. Our cave at one time had sheltered the Ku Klux Klan.

That moment, staring down at the moldered hood, I heard my daddy proclaiming the Nigger Rule.

Malcolm and I made Black Bob our own private fort. In dribbles, we toted our best things there: comic books (*Captain Marvel, Archie, Bat Man, Superman*); baseball cards, which we'd swapped so many times the players' uniforms were grubby and thinned; matches; Co'-Colas and a church key to open them; Barnum's Animals Crackers in boxes like zoo cages. It crossed my mind to bring Fats—so we could practice the bones—but I decided against that. It'd be impossible to keep the ol' bone man still during a skeleton-napping from home. Instead, I lugged *Gray's Anatomy* back and forth. It was weighty but quiet. The bone names weren't a leadpipe cinch for Malcolm, but he got them pretty quick. Me, sometimes I thought they'd just bust my brain.

I brought along my bowie knife—the present from Daddy when I turned ten. You never knew, I reasoned, when you'd need such a weapon. Like a moth, the Klan flitted through my mind. But they were long gone from Black Bob.

Our fort set Malcolm's imagination afire.

"Hey, David," he said one time, eyes sparking, "let's be cavemen."

"Great!" I said right off. I wished I'd thought of that.

For tinder, we gathered dry leaves, in huge armfuls light as breaths. We tossed on twigs. When the heap was the right size, I tried to light it. *Fssst. Fssst. Fssst.* The soggy matches fizzled out. Finally, a tiny flame flared.

"Ugnh," Malcolm grunted, leaping all over with wild excitement, even though you had to squint to see the flame. He was Caveman Malcolm, who'd just now stumbled upon fire.

"Ugnh," I grunted back.

I cupped my hands around the flare and blew on it gently, so's not to snuff it.

We had some hot dogs I'd filched from our icebox. It wasn't a burn-in-hell sin, I reckoned. Sooner or later I'd have eaten them at home. We stuck the hot dogs on oak sticks and charred them once we got a blaze going. Their juice sizzled in the fire. The aroma made my belly gurgle. "Ungh! Ungh! Oogh! Ongh!" Malcolm and I delighted ourselves. We were cavemen. We made cave paintings, fire-ash smears on the walls.

We grunted and snorted our way through that autumn day. We thought we sounded like real-true ancient men. Most likely we sounded like hogs.

It was in Black Bob Cave that I first felt the devil, old Beelzebub himself, blurt through my lips. Maybe it happened on account of the dark. Or the mystery of the cave itself.

"Goddamn!" I suddenly said. The word rang against the damp cave walls as if from some great stone anvil.

"Goddamn!" It rolled off my tongue, with the glassy beauty of an aggie marble. I felt a power that probably most boys—and girls—had felt since the Beginning. I cussed again.

Malcolm embellished on it.

"Goddammit to hell!" he roared happily.

"Shitpail!" I roared.

"Shittruck!" Malcolm roared back.

"Shitwagon!"

Oh! Sweet ruination!

I listened to the gorgeous reverberations, soon swallowed down the old cave's throat. In my own house, if I'd attempted such blasphemy, my daddy would've whipped the tar outta me. But there, with Malcolm, I was safe.

Our cursing mingled with the other echoes in Black Bob. They probably still quiver somewhere there, in the old and redeeming dark.

One afternoon at Black Bob it was raining heavily, rinsing the world so it shone like new. Rain dripped from the dark mouth of the cave. It pecked at the ground. It drummed through the trees, making a mush of the leaves. All around us rose the rank stink of Confederate piss and damp comic books. Malcolm and I were stuck in the cave for a time, unless we wanted to get sodden slogging home in that storm. It was then Malcolm noticed my bowie knife, resting on a pile of comics.

"Hey," he said suddenly. "Wanna be blood brothers?" There was never a doubt in my mind. The movies guided us on how this was done. Malcolm and I loved the picture shows, especially Westerns. Roy Rogers, Gene Autry, Lash LaRue, Hopalong Cassidy, the Cisco Kid, Hoot Gibson, they were our heroes—real men who loved their horses and never kissed girls if they could help it and who brought justice to all with their fists.

Both Malcolm and I had witnessed scenes in cowboy pictures in which white men and Indians solemnly became blood brothers. Forevermore sworn to come running at the drop of a Stetson hat or a war bonnet. To help each other out of every jam, till the absolute end of time.

A solemn ceremony began. Once it did, it flowed, easy as blood.

We squatted on the ground. We rested our arms next to each other on the Georgia Belle peach crate that was our table. His arm was warm, I remember. Malcolm picked up the bowie.

"I'll do the slittin'," he said.

"No," I said. "I will."

"Come on," he said, running his thumb gingerly along the edge.

"No, it's my knife."

"Shoot, David," he grumbled, but he gave in.

So I did the slitting instead. The knife was razor sharp. "Ready?"

"Ready." His eyes looked brave.

Carefully, I nicked Malcolm's forearm. When the metal first touched him, he tightened his fist, but he never squealed. We both watched the blood puddle bloom.

Then I nicked myself. I was overeager, so the cut went

deeper than I'd planned. I sucked air when the blade bit in.

"Quick," I said. "Arms together."

Our two blood puddles touched. Mingled. Red and sticky and metallic smelling and warm. Neither of us spoke. I waited for Malcolm's blood to mix with mine. For my eyes to flash like his. For his spunk to take hold of me.

"Blood brothers. Salt and pepper. Friends forever."

Suddenly, Malcolm said those words. "Now you say it, David."

"Blood brothers. Salt and pepper. Friends forever."

Then for a time it was perfectly still inside Black Bob Cave. Perfectly peaceful. Except for the hymn of the rain.

Though I'd pressed damp leaves to my arm, when I got home, the cut was still bleeding. My doctoring wasn't yet up to stanching it.

"What's this?" my daddy asked with concern.

"A cut."

"It's a mean one. How'd you get it?"

"Oh, messin' round," I fudged. "Mighta been a nail."

"Sit there, son. Don't budge. And never fear—yore daddy The Leech is nigh." My daddy enjoyed referring to himself as The Leech because old-time doctors laid on bloodsuckers to cure the sick.

Right quick, he got his medical valise and swabbed the

wound with iodine, which stung. Then he took a couple
of small stitches in my arm. Like Grandmother Church
doing cross-stitch, he was a real artist.

"This'll burn some," he said before poking the needle
in. Then he injected me against the tetanus.

I didn't feel a hurt. I felt glad. I knew that I had within
me some of Malcolm's blood.

Daddy never learned the truth about my wound. Boys
will be boys, he'd said. I had a mysterious cut, that was
all. If he'd ever had any inkling how I'd gotten it, he'd
have turned purple and yelled, "Jesus Christ, Lord God
A'mighty, you're tainted with nigger blood!"

Then, sure as hell, Daddy would've murdered us.

10.

Malcolm and I had been blood brothers for a time when Uncle Lucas paid a visit. Lucas lived up North, near Boston. In the state he called "Massatoosutts."

Sometimes I'd write him a letter to his house on Pantry Road; right soon, he'd send me a letter back. He'd always enclose a two-dollar bill because he thought that was one right smart currency. And because Thomas Jefferson'd been a redhead like him.

I thought it was right smart, too. I liked the conspirational look of ol' Tom, staring out at me from beneath his bushy eyebrows. Seemed like he had something important to talk over with me—in private, probably about the running of the government.

My Uncle Lucas loved to sing. Like a mockingbird, he warbled any tune he heard, from the holy to the coarse. He belted lyrics like, "We were dancing in the dark and goosin' statues in the park . . ." (which curled my grandmother's blue hair). He favored songs like "The Tennessee Waltz" and "Jambalaya" and "Wabash Cannonball" and "In the Jailhouse Now," where he'd been a time or two, and in particular "The Great Speckle Bird," about the Bible and God's holy word. "Nobody knows its origin," Uncle Lucas once told me, "but it's a damn fine song." "Speckle Bird" was made famous by Roy Acuff on the Grand Ole Opry. When my uncle performed it, he became Roy Acuff, it seemed to me, afloat on the beauty of the notes.

Uncle Lucas was a figure cloaked in romance. His business was import and export. I wasn't any more clear on that than I was about the meaning of Methodist. The work took him to far-off lands like China and Indonesia and Japan and France. But sometimes it brought him back to us.

My imagination performed gyrations, and I wondered if something else kept him away.

Like the unforeseen arrival of a solitary bird, one evening Uncle Lucas appeared on our porch.

"Somebody come open up this damn door," he bellowed, "'fore I kick it in!"

Nobody cursed like Uncle Lucas. Funny, I thought, that somebody could cuss like blue blazes and still be godly. I rushed downstairs and let him in. His ox-body nearly filled the porch. His arms, like two hairy hams, were heaped with presents, which I hoped were mostly for me. His red hair, swooping past his ears like hot licks of flame, bounced, and his red beard flared like the pirate Barbarossa's.

"What child is this before me?" he thundered. "Cain't be David. David's a runt. Where's David? He's the one I wanna see!" He began searching the parlor. Under the sofa cushions and the ottoman, inside the chifforobe.

"Hey, Uncle Lucas," I said softly. "It's me."

"You foolin' with me?"

"No sir."

"A proof! We need a proof!" He grinned, his teeth like a whole set of ivory dominoes lined up.

Lucas leaned close. "How d' ya spell 'rat'?" he asked.

'Course, I knew the family joke about our Southern speech for "right" and grinned. "R-a-t," I said, "as in 'rat now.'"

He gave a suspicious squint. "You got that one, but still you might could be a spy. If you know the words to this song, you're my nephew, David Church. If you don't, I'll notify Sheriff Roy Hyde. 'Cause you're a good-for-nothin' deceitful bandit intent upon burglary."

Uncle Lucas roared "The Animal Fair," which went in part like this:

> *The monkey, he got drunk,*
> *and fell on the elephant's trunk.*
> *The elephant sneezed and fell to his knees,*
> *so that was the end of the monk, the monk, the monk.*

It was my favorite song, so I chimed right in.

"Well now, I reckon you passed the David Test." Then Uncle Lucas embraced me. Like a vise.

"Lucas." Grandmother Church was there.

"Mama."

They hugged as if taking a long drink of water. Daddy came in. "Hello, Lucas, you ol' revenant." He shook his hand, a speck stiffly it seemed to me.

Grandmother Church believed Uncle Lucas was drunk as a skunk whenever he sang the monkey song.

"You're a snowball headed for hell," she whispered, looking sheepish, surely about uttering a bad word.

"Yes'm," said Lucas.

But I didn't believe he was damned, not for one hot little minute.

Once my daddy and grandmother had told Lucas umpteen-ump times what a low-down scalawag he was for neither corresponding nor in any way informing them of his whereabouts, they fed him to popping and sat him down and listened to his blab.

A lull came and Uncle Lucas said, "Here, David, hold out your hand."

When I did, he set a box on my palm. It was like an undersize brick, made entirely of wood with a fancy design.

"What is it?" I asked.

"A chimpanzee."

"Quit funnin' me."

"Okay. In reality, this is," he whispered loudly behind his hand, "a genuine Chinese trick box."

"Just what the doctor ordered," said Daddy. "A Chink-box."

Grandmother Church drew a sharp breath.

"Franklin," Uncle Lucas said quietly, "don't spoil it for the boy."

I was so excited, I hardly heard my daddy's words. The gift sounded wonderfully mysterious. I studied it for some time, but could not guess its purpose.

"What does it do?" I asked at last.

Uncle Lucas pulled me onto the screened porch.

"Watch real careful," he told me. "Secret agents could be closin' in on us, so I'm showin' you only this once."

But before he could demonstrate its inner workings, Slur Tucker staggered onto our porch, stinking like a sour rag. He hadn't been swiggin' soda pop, that's for damn sure. I yelped, repelled by the sight of him. At sometime or other, Slur had got the cancer, so a doctor had to cut out a hunk of his nose. It never healed properly, Daddy said. A little oozy yellow bandage always clung to the tip of Slur's nose, like a tiny and hideous quilt patch. Slur stared at us stupidly for a minute, then hawked a nasty glob onto the lawn. I looked away right quick, on account of his evil powers.

"Yore daddy roun'?" He slobbered out the words, running his tongue over his scummy teeth. A little blub of spittle clung to his chin.

"Inside," Uncle Lucas growled.

"Thank 'e kindly, Loo-cuss." He belched and grinned drunkenly.

If he couldn't just make an angel sweat!

Uncle Lucas gave him a look that could've cooked down steel before Daddy opened up and Slur lurched inside the house.

"He's so full o' spirits, you could put a cork in that no-account an' sell 'im as rotgut," Lucas said.

Why in the world was that hateful bum Daddy's friend? Slur was a drunk. And he was Klan. Everybody knew it. Soon as he'd stumbled away, I felt like snapping up a stiff brush and scouring down the spot where he'd been swaying.

"Uncle Lucas?" I asked. "What's Daddy doin', hanging round him?"

Uncle Lucas looked at me. "Don' know, David," he said, his voice soaked in gloom. "I just don' know." I thought he did. I thought I knew, too. And I hated what I thought.

I wondered if that was what took Lucas up North.

"Daddy won't let my friend Malcolm in the house," I said. "He deserves to come in more than that trash Tucker. Think sometime Daddy'll change his mind?"

I was close on tears. Uncle Lucas took my face in his great big hands. He looked at me long. Then he said gently, "Don't set your heart on it, David."

❖ ❖ ❖

The trick box looked solid, but its surfaces were made up of small slabs of wood, each about as thick as a stick of gum. Certain of the slabs, Uncle Lucas revealed, slid. Should a person know which ones those were, and should a person know the order in which those slabs should slip, well, that fortunate person could *open* the Chinese trick box.

Uncle Lucas and I crouched beneath the porch light like two gigantic night bugs. With all the stealth that was inside his big frame, he slid those particular sides for me. Slowly. Tantalizingly. One by one by one by one. I nearly fainted from the waiting.

"Open Sezme." His voice rang like a gong.

The lid of the little box slid open.

Something had happened. I felt different. I felt like being quiet. In all the world, only my uncle and I shared this secret.

How could I sleep? I knew a secret. I'd never tell a soul—except Malcolm.

In the quiet of my room, I practiced the moves that would open the small wooden brick. Over and over, so I'd never forget. When I knew them like the days of the week, I opened the Chinese trick box. I folded up something and put it inside. It was a poem:

Malcolm. He's my brother.
His eyes spark like the devil.
He can piss a whole lot
farther than me.
And he knows the bone names.
I love him.

II.

Early one Sunday morning, Daddy backed the Buick from the garage and took a long look at it. It must have had a film of dust.

"David," he called, crooking a finger at me, "come on over here. You need to wash this automobile before we go to church."

I glanced at the car. It looked fine to me. But there was no use quibbling with Daddy.

"Hop to it," he said. "You call me when it's ready. We don't wanna be late."

"We don't?" I muttered.

I lugged a pail of warm, soapy water from the house down to the driveway. The bucket was heavy, so I struggled it along. Going down the porch steps, I steadied it against one leg, careful not to slosh any.

To apply the soapsuds I used a chamois, which had to be clean as a sultan's undergarments (if a sultan wore undergarments), according to Daddy. I dipped the chamois into the suds and wrung it out a few times, enjoying the slimy feel of the thing. Then I worked section by section, rinsing each one with water from the garden hose when I was done. After that, I rinsed out the chamois real well and gave the entire car a pass-over to get rid of the glaze of water. Finally, I dried each part with a tired towel, equally clean as a sultan's drawers and soft as a baby's behind.

For the chrome I used a special polish, the color of Pepto-Bismol. Each time I poured a dab of the liquid onto my polishing rag, the can it was in gave a little hollow gulp. I let the polish dry to a pink crust, then removed it with a spotless flannel cloth, a swatch from my worn-out Roy Rogers pajamas.

Though I knew Daddy expected the Buick to be spick-'n'-span, I tried to work fast 'cause he was in a fret to get going.

To make the job go quicker, I pretended the Buick was the rare and oversize Brazilian slick-back beetle, the only one known to mankind. And that I was cleaning it up for a world-famous scientist to put on display in his laboratory. I was pleased with my leaping imagination, which I was for-ever trying to develop to be as flamboyant as Malcolm's.

First off, I washed the beetle's right wing; then the left. I swabbed the creature's head (the grill was the mouth) and its behind (the rear bumper). I got up on the kitchen ladder, which I'd borrowed from my grandmother, to scrub the convertible top, the big bug's back. After that, I homed in on the windows, working them into my bug-picture as see-through segments of the insect's vitals that made it lighter and helped it fly faster. I rubbed clean the long blub of a hood ornament, the snout. Last of all came the whitewalls, which were the beetle's feet. There would have been six if the car were a common insect, but the Brazilian slick-back crawled along on but four.

It took me a good while to complete the chore. When I was satisfied, I called out, "Daddy, I'm done."

Daddy came out and checked my work like a drill sergeant scrutinizes bunks for mitered corners and wrinkles and lumps. He strolled all around the Buick. Then he took out a clean white handkerchief and ran it slowly over the automobile's black flanks.

He peered close and made a dark little noise in his throat. "What's this here, David?"

I stood beside him and looked. I could see only the gleam of a Brazilian beetle wing.

"I don't know."

"Well, look closer." Daddy's voice took on an edge.

I squinted. But for the life of me I couldn't see a fool thing. "I don't know, sir."

"Horse collar! It's lint, David." He looked at me, head cocked like a mean little bird, and said, "This is a half-ass job if I ever saw one. Do it again, sonny boy."

He dumped the bucket of scummy suds over the car, then walked back into the house.

I washed the car again. And again. While I worked I

boiled about Daddy. How I'd have liked to swap him for somebody else.

After three tries, I called him once more to inspect my work.

"Well now, that's a right smart job, David," Daddy said, grinning widely and replacing his handkerchief in his suit pocket.

He packed the family into the Buick. He slipped the car into gear, let out the clutch, and eased out of the driveway. Though we were late, he drove off calmly.

So, I thought, the devil is driving to church.

12.

One day in that same year, Miss Grace Bando, down the street, sent for me by way of her part-time girl Zora. Zora knew my daddy's stand on Negroes. Everybody in our town did. So when I answered the doorbell, she stood so far back on the porch, one more step and she'd have tumbled down backward.

"Mornin', Mr. David. Miss Grace'd be obliged to see you rat now." *R-a-t, as in "rat now."* I thought of our family joke and grinned. Zora let go of the words in a flurry. Before I could blurt a reply, she was flurrying herself back to the safety of Miss Grace's.

By coincidence, or probably because he was always hanging around, Malcolm came by at that time.

"Hey, David," he said, eyes lit with mischief, "let's go glue us a nickel to the sidewalk and hide and see who we can fool."

Normally I'd have loved to watch our neighbors peek secretively over their shoulders, then stoop to prize a glued coin from the pavement. Then we could compare the sizes of their backsides and learn who cussed best. Not today. We'd had a call from Miss Grace.

"Somethin' better's come up," I said. "Job's waiting on us."

"Yeah? What?"

"Don' know. But," I spoke real slow, as though my tongue were bogged in molasses, "it's offered by . . . *Miss Grace Bando*."

"Well, git a *move* on!" We sprinted for her place.

Miss Grace was a Daughter of the Confederacy. She had numerous male relatives who'd fought and died or had fought and been maimed in the Civil War. The Recent Unpleasantness, she termed it. Though the war had ended over eighty years before, to honor those men, she moved in gowns of black crepe, like dark swishing water. (Miss Grace's black crepe dresses were only of the finest quality: "You owe it to your friends to look nice" was her motto.)

Charles Henry Bando, her great-grandfather, had lost his right arm at the bloody Battle of Shiloh. It had been, according to scuttlebutt, "slashed off by a Yankee saber just below the elbow, though not before Bando had wounded a passel of enemy scum." To keep the memory of his war years aflame, Charles Henry Bando had ordered his severed appendage preserved like a bass by the finest taxidermist in Memphis. The grisly relic, rumor had it, was hidden from ever-vengeful Yankees, stored with reverence someplace at Miss Grace's residence.

Once Malcolm and I'd got wind of this, we fixed us a lifetime goal: to get us a look at that arm. We spent considerable time mumbling about it, like two eggs aboil in water.

"Wonder where the damn thing is," I said to Malcolm.

"Put yourself in her spot," he'd suggested once. "Where'd you hide a stuffed arm?"

"To hide it from anybody? Or from you and me?"

"From us, o' course," Malcolm said. "Shoot, David, nobody can think twistier."

The pull of the arm was great. We hung around Miss Grace's house with high expectations. Our desire was fervent—we simply *had* to see the thing or expire in the attempt.

One evening my daddy was making a house call. I was supposed to be boning up with Fats, who now hung from a big iron hook by the headboard of my bed, a fedora like Daddy's atop his skull, a bow tie slung around his neck. Instead of boning up, I slipped out to meet Malcolm.

"No talking," I whispered.

"No talking," mouthed Malcolm.

Our scheme, concocted in advance, was to scout the outside of Miss Grace's place. Maybe the old girl'd hid the relic there. Maybe she was more devious than we'd given her credit for.

We cloud-walked up. Cloud-walking was a thing Malcolm's mama had taught him, a way of moving, real soft, like a cloud might walk, if it cared to.

Then Malcolm and I skulked around the old house, alert as deer. The later it got, the spookier the place seemed.

Shadows began creeping in on us. I listened sharp, and there were sounds I noticed that I hadn't heard before. The trees lurking, their skeleton branches rubbing, like bone on bone. I shivered inside but didn't let on. Malcolm would've snorted at me for a coward—it took a hell of a lot more than trees to scare him.

First off, we checked the garage, where Miss Grace kept a '40 Chevy. It was locked with a padlock the size of a fist. With burglar stealth, we sidled around it, checking every inch. It seemed there was no place to put an old arm. Like a possum finding my nighttime sight, I squinted and peered all around. Suddenly, I *knew*, I knew exactly where the swag was stashed. I poked Malcolm.

"What?"

I pointed vigorously to the side of the main house, at the drainpipe that ran from the roof to the ground. Malcolm shot me a look of pure pity. "She'da had to run the arm through the meat grinder, to fit in there," he said with scorn.

"Shoot." I felt deflated.

It was then we heard it—a sound like a sprung door, then something shuffling in the bushes, right close.

"What's *that*?" I swallowed my gum. Starting at the tip and slowly creeping up, my backbone froze into one long icicle.

"Dunno," whispered Malcolm.

"You s'pose ol' Grace's a shooter?" I asked, though I'd never seen her armed.

Malcolm and I didn't wait to find out. We ran like a jail-break. After that, we focused our energy on the inside of Miss Grace's house. Every time she needed a chore done, we came, full of hope, on the run.

"Hello, boys," Miss Grace said morosely the day she'd sent Zora to fetch us.

Miss Grace Bando was a heavy little woman. Mostly bosom. Built like a hen. Usually she greeted us like a hen, too. Not fluttery, but friendly and warm. Malcolm and I'd decided that was on account of she didn't have children of her own. She seemed to love anybody lively and young.

Miss Grace was in a real swivet and kept fiddling with a frilly handkerchief. "Something terrible has befallen me. It's brought on a *crise du fois*. That's French for 'liver crisis.'"

Immediately, I imagined the worst—the famous Confederate stump had been filched, purloined, stolen. I felt my whole face slump.

"Oh," I said, my voice barely moving air.

"You boys'd better come on in." Like it was nothing to invite Malcolm.

We entered Miss Grace's parlor and sat down on the settee. Because she was tiny, Miss Grace had to hop up onto it. Her little feet dangled high above the parquet floor.

The room was dim and choked with heavy furniture. It contained as much paraphernalia as Pruett's dry-goods store. Every table had a little lamp on it, with a beaded fringe, like a glowing jellyfish.

I was trying to be on my best manners, but it was an effort. Hope is the one thing that can't be completely snuffed out. Though certain the arm had been pilfered, I couldn't help but scan around, fiddling the while with the beading of a jellyfish lamp. My eyes searched the dark niches of the parlor. I was betting Malcolm was doing the same.

When that tack failed, I started sniffing, taking an olfactory approach to flushing out the arm.

"David, what's come over you? Stop that sniffing," said Miss Grace. "Pay attention."

"Uh—yes'm."

"It's Gethsemane."

"What?"

"The crisis."

"Shoot, that's too bad." I swallowed a smile.

Gethsemane was Miss Grace's sow, a pig of magnificent size. About as big around as a water tank and white as a bowl of milk. Evenings, I sometimes caught sight of the bulky Geth rooting through our yard for some tasty morsel, snuffling pleasantly.

"Yesterday, she set out on one of her garden tours, but she still hasn't returned. Will you-all fetch her home?"

I liked Miss Grace. And I liked her sow. I was happy to go try to retrieve her.

"Sure," I said.

"Sure," said Malcolm.

"Both you-all will get a dollar."

To some, that was probably a piddly-ass amount of money. To us, it was a bonanza. I tried to appear nonchalant, imagining the comic books and Bazooka bubble gum and baseball cards I could buy with my half of that sum.

"That's fair," Malcolm said.

"Real fair," I agreed.

We were halfway out the front door when Miss Grace called, "Hold on!" She handed us each a gnarled yam. "To lure my baby home."

"Don't fret, Miss Grace, we're professional sow catchers," Malcolm said, eyes agleam.

"Don't fret, Miss Grace," I chimed in. "It's only a matter of time."

Before we left, I glanced around the parlor again. Not an arm in sight. *Damn!*

Malcolm and I dashed down Cherokee Street, each holding a yam like we were shaking hands with a tree root. My eyes were peeled for Gethsemane. She was big and white, so she'd be hard to miss.

As we went along, I hooted something I'd learned in kindergarten, only I'd changed the words some:

"Goin' on a sow hunt. Gonna catch a big one. I'm not scared. It's a be-oo-ti-ful day."

Malcolm jumped right in. We turned the corner and hollered our way down Bonner Street, cutting through yards to save time. None of the neighbors seemed to mind. They smiled or laughed and wished us luck. Mrs. Purvis looked up from the bed of four-o'clocks she was salting for snails. (Not a whole box of Morton's, just enough to shrivel 'em up without withering her flowers.)

"Y'all catch a big one, now, hear?"

"Gonna catch us a *huge* one!" I sang back.

It was a be-oo-ti-ful day. Malcolm and I spent it inspecting gardens. Now and then we came upon the small plowings of a pig. But not the pig herself. That Gethsemane was a slippery one. Eluded us all day.

When I tired of the song, I called her like a dog.

"Here, Geth! Here, Geth-Geth-Geth!"

"You knucklehead," said Malcolm, "you gotta call her like a *pig*."

He commenced to squeal like a banshee queen. "Sooo-eee! Sooo-eee! Pig! Pig! Pig!"

I heard a rustle in the Ropers' rhododendrons. "Hush up!" I said. I could nearly feel the crinkle of paper money in my hand. Eagerly, I peeped into the bushes. "Geth?"

A filthy face peered back. Scared the holy wad out of me. It was the Mole Man.

The Mole Man roamed the streets of our town on a rickety old bicycle, ringing the little bell and calling out, "What's yo' killin' wants? What's yo' killin' needs?" The rusted handlebars were slung with traps and cages full of dead rodents—gophers and squirrels and moles and such—like a weird Christmas-tree branch.

To me the Mole Man was a marvelous mystery, inviting deliriums of imagination. I figured him for a crazed killer who'd served his time and was now scot-free. He could at any moment give up the murdering of moles and return to murdering men. That was what I thought before I talked to Uncle Lucas.

"Who's the Mole Man?" I'd asked him once. Lucas didn't hold anything against dark people. I knew he'd give me a fair answer. Still, he could embroider a tale like nobody's business. With ghoulish eagerness, I waited for the worst.

"He's a man who'd thought to become a doctor, like you," Lucas said. "Till he learned that colored men best not have dreams. So he switched his focus to drinking. And killing moles an' other vermin. Two bits apiece."

This information worked on me like the turn of a kaleidoscope. One moment, I'd had the Mole Man pegged as a cutthroat. A dangerous loon. The next, a great sadness swept over me, like a great gray wave off the sea.

Malcolm spanged into my mind.

"How come a Negro can't dream?"

"'Cause, David, it's the white man's boat we're afloat in. A person who rocks it, well, he could get hurt."

"You mean . . . the Klan?"

It was the first time I'd ever uttered the word. I shuddered. Like the very saying of it might conjure them up.

"Klan—or anybody who hates. Some men just need to keep ahead by keepin' a foot on another's neck." Uncle Lucas's voice was dark. By the sound, he was talking about a particular dream crusher.

A horrible inkling ran through me and I shuddered. I began thinking on who that somebody might be.

"Don't you ever call him the Mole Man, David," Uncle Lucas said. "You call him Mister Swann. That's his name."

Well now. That was something to know. Like everything that took place, I told Malcolm.

"Hello, Mister Swann," I said when I'd recovered from my fright.

"Hello, Mister Swann," said Malcolm.

The gaunt old man wore a tattered shirt, grubby coveralls, and a filthy billed cap that tilted on his head at a jaunty angle. His shoes were unmatched. He smelled as though he never washed. He smelled like dirt. And moles. Maybe that wasn't such a bad thing. A saying spranged into my mind: God made the dirt; the dirt don't hurt.

Mister Swann also smelled of liquor. Tarantula juice, Uncle Lucas called it. He tipped his cap.

"A mole," he said, dangling a small, limp body by the tail. Its bright eyes stared. Its tiny teeth were bared in a permanent snarl. "Could you use a mole today?" Mister Swann's voice was high, a choir boy's falsetto.

The creature was an offering. A show that he liked us.

"No, thank you, Mister Swann," I said politely. "But we *could* use a sow. A live one," I emphasized. "We're hunting Gethsemane."

Mister Swann's eyes glazed over. "That's a garden," he said. "Bad un."

Gethsemane was the place where Jesus was betrayed.

"Don't remember no pig bein' there," Mister Swann said, puzzled. Then, as if on cue, the canny sow materialized from a bush, nuzzling up to me. On account of the yam in my hand.

"Hey, Geth," I said, patting her barrel-body. "Let's git on home, ol' girl."

I don't know what Malcolm was thinking about, but I was thinking partly of the money we'd earned. And partly of how pleased Miss Grace would be to see her Gethsemane. I was also thinking about the ragged man before me.

I picked up a pebble from the yard. From where Mister Swann had stood. It was streaked with grime from his shoes. When I got home, I'd put the pebble in my trick box.

The sun was beginning to set. Malcolm and I had started for Miss Grace's, yams held just ahead of Gethsemane's snout. She followed them at a lumbering trot, snorting like some busted-up piece of farm equipment. I turned to see what Mister Swann was doing. In a rustle, he dragged his bicycle from the shrubbery. He placed a dead mole into one of the cages. Tenderly. He lashed the cage to the handlebars and fumbled onto the seat. I paused and raised my hand in salute. Malcolm did, too. Mister Swann raised his hand toward us. Then, hunched over the handlebars, with a thin metal shiver from his bicycle, he wobbled down Cherokee Street.

"What's yo' killin' wants?" he chanted mournfully. "What's yo' killin' needs?"

For a moment the coppery glow of the sun held him in molten outline, like melted pennies poured over his shoulders.

13.

Fats the skeleton was my mentor. When I wasn't at real school or playing someplace with Malcolm, I studied on him, on all the little tags hung from his frame. My future dangled from his bones. If I could just keep those bones straight in my head—plus vocabulary words and a few thousand other items Daddy had in mind—I'd hold the Barlow Academy in my grasp.

Daddy knew my favorite was the lazy bone, but I didn't know his. So one time I asked him, "Daddy, what's your favorite bone?"

"Hyoid, hands down."

"Why?"

"It's a floater. The only one not connected to the rest."

"What's it like?"

"Small, squarish. Like a little horseshoe."

"What's it do?"

"It rests at the root of the tongue," my daddy said. "Supports the tongue and its workings."

"So it's the talking bone?"

"You could say that." We laughed.

My daddy told me about when he was in school, studying medicine. An instructor had shown his class a painting, a still life from a time way back in history. The Renaissance, maybe. Daddy was fuzzy about that. Anyhow, in the picture was a skeleton, all connected to itself. Except for one bone, lying on a table. That bone was the hyoid, "a bone apart."

"Did you know, David, to learn how bodies were put together, artists at that time stole out at dead of night and dug up graves?"

"They *did?*"

"Or they bribed somebody in the morgue to let them perform their dissections," Daddy said. "They got caught, they died, or were tortured at the very least."

Till then I had no idea art was such a dangerous business. The thought awoke my blood lust. The morgue. In my mind I called up visions of the pallid dead, laid out on tables row upon row, like wax candles. Their mouths were closed, holding on to words they'd never let go of.

Right then I set myself another goal: to visit the morgue and view a dead body, "worm food" to Malcolm and me. I just wanted to see, like going to the picture shows. Jeez! Maybe—if everything worked out—maybe Malcolm could come, too! I didn't hold my breath on that one.

Malcolm and I talked about a morgue trip sometimes. We'd describe to each other in gruesome detail the look of the place, and the stench of it. Then, for total effect, we'd bray what we called "The Mortifying Body Song":

Did you ever think when a hearse goes by
  that you might be the next to die?
They wrap you up in a big white sheet
  and throw you down about six feet deep.
You'll be all right for about a week,
  but then your coffin begins to leak.
Your body turns a slimy green.
  The pus squirts out like shaving cream.
The worms crawl in, the worms crawl out,
  the worms play pinochle on your snout.
They eat your eyes, they eat your nose,
  they eat the jelly between your toes.

Those were all the words we knew, all we needed to know, to ghoul up the morgue in our minds.

"Can I visit the morgue, Daddy?"

My daddy looked at me. "Not just yet, son," he said.

"Why?"

"You're young. Green. You'll need to get toughened some."

"By what?"

Daddy didn't have an answer for that.

Life is a kaleidoscope, like I said. One minute things seem one way; next minute clicks you up a whole new picture. That's how it was with the bones. At first it was fun trying to learn them. But truth was, a lot of times when I wanted to go play, I had to stay home to study on Fats. Daddy set up a quota of names for me to learn each week. Then he drilled me on them again and again, till sometimes I thought I'd just scream.

But you didn't scream, not with him.

I had a hell of a time learning the names. It wasn't that my mind was a colander exactly. And I surely had desire. But there were so many, some so like others, and some so strange: *clavicle, patella, humerus, tibia, phalanges*. Who named the damn things? They just hung before me like a puzzle, as if those ol' hunks of ossification were trying to trick me on purpose.

Just when I thought I had them, Daddy'd toss something else into the soup pot of learning, like blood vessels or the cranial nerves. As a memory aid, from the beginning letters of those nerves, I worked me up a delicious word: *OOOTTAFAGVAH. OOOTTAFAGVAH* helped me a lot.

I thought about how Malcolm soaked up this stuff pretty easily when we fooled around in the cave. Hey, that could impress Daddy—a kaleidoscope click that might get Malcolm inside my house.

"Guess what?" Fudging a little, I suddenly plunged in one time. "Malcolm knows all the bones."

I waited for Daddy to be amazed.

He looked at me and his eyes were glass.

Daddy said, "You're a friggin' liar."

❖ ❖ ❖

My daddy wanted me to learn real bad.

"What's this one?" he asked me one night. I didn't answer right off, so his voice sharpened up.

"David, what is it?" I tightened inside and my mind froze and no bone names came. Not a one.

"Well now," Daddy said. "You best bear down, sonny boy. Age thirteen's just round the bend."

He paused and studied me for a long minute. I felt sickish. Now it was coming.

"Know something? Learning the bones was hard for me, too."

My mouth dropped open.

"Yessir. Came to keeping them in my cranium, I was a real bonehead." He guffawed at the joke.

"Hey, David, I know what."

"What?"

"Let's go get us a speck o' something to help you think. And you, sir, stay put," he told Fats as we left my room, headed downstairs.

"What helps you think?" I asked.

Daddy scanned the kitchen. "Devil's food cake," he said. "Best brain food in Christendom."

"How come you know that?"

"Don't second-guess me, boy." He sparkled. "I'm yore daddy, The Leech."

14.

Daddy had a friend, Jimmy Bee. And he was dying. Of the colon cancer. Jimmy and Daddy'd grown up together on Cherokee Street. Every evening during the late stage of Jimmy's sickness, Daddy went down the block to check on him.

From early on, Daddy often took me with him on house calls. "So you can get the feel of it," he told me. By this time, I was pretty used to the sick. But not to dying people.

One evening, my daddy and I rapped on the Bees' door. After a time, his wife opened it and motioned us in.

"How is he?" Daddy asked right off.

"In considerable pain," Mrs. Bee said. "You know the way." She nodded toward the stairs.

"Thank you, Emeline."

Just outside the bedroom door, Daddy stopped and crouched down so he could look into my eyes. He said, "No matter how bad it seems, don't be alarmed, David. Dying's a natural thing. At the far side of birth. At some time or other, those two come round and meet—like a circle closing. Like we go back to where we start."

As we entered, I willed myself not to be scared.

You could tell Mrs. Bee'd done her best to brighten the bedroom. On the nightstand was a little lamp, glowing in the gloom. It was trying so hard to be cheerful, the lamp looked sad. And there was a vase with a bunch of honeysuckle in it. Despite their fragrance, a peculiar odor clung to everything. When Daddy closed the door, the curtain moved and I shivered. I imagined Death lurking behind it.

A bright green comforter lay over Jimmy's dozing form. It covered him only partly, and as I got closer, I saw that his pajama top was splashed with yellowy vomit, down the front. His mouth was open. He stunk pretty bad and I gagged. Then I breathed through my mouth and played like things were normal, to spare Jimmy's feelings, should he waken.

Daddy paused. "You okay, son?"

"I'm okay."

Daddy started cleaning Jimmy up, talking to him all the while.

"Hey, Jimmy, it's me, Franklin, The Leech. How ya doin'?"

His eyes opened, and he gave Daddy a limp something that could have passed for a grin. "Been better."

Daddy peeled off the soiled clothing. He filled up a porcelain basin with warm water from a little washstand on one wall. "David," he said as he bathed Jimmy gently

with a washcloth, "fetch me a fresh top." While he toweled off Jimmy, he pointed to the chest of drawers. I slid each drawer open quietly as I could till I found the right one. I took out a pajama top, light blue with thin navy stripes, and took it to Daddy.

"Put it on him, son."

Daddy propped Jimmy up while I struggled him into the garment. When I touched him, he felt damp and fevered, and all bone. No weight to him. Like Fats. Like he was already gone. Though changing the clothing seemed a small thing, it took all of Jimmy's effort. He sighed deeply and sank down, like a balloon emptied of its air.

Daddy smoothed the bedsheets and began talking. As if it were thirty years before, and they were still boys. "'Member the tunnel we dug with spoons in the lot next to King Akin's house? Took us most of that summer. Smelled of worms and dark. Our flashlight was treasonous. Sputtered. We took our good stuff down there."

Jimmy didn't speak, but he nodded. Like he was back in some otherwhere.

Daddy talked on and on, holding Jimmy's hand.

One time, Jimmy said, "Franklin, I'd like a drink."

Water, I thought, hopping up. But no. Daddy opened up the little nightstand door and pulled out a bottle. He poured a slug into an eyewash glass and lifted the whiskey to Jimmy's lips.

"Tennessee?" he asked weakly. As if any other type would be mortal.

"Tennessee," said my daddy.

I must've looked surprised.

"Why deprive the man?" Daddy said later on. "He's dyin'."

That evening, I learned more about doctoring than I ever did again. More than ever, I wanted to be like Daddy.

Not long after, Daddy brought some news home.

"Mama, Jimmy's gone," Daddy said, entering the house one afternoon and closing the door quietly behind him. He didn't wait for her to speak. "I was sitting beside him, thinking on my plans for tomorrow, when the last breath whispered out of him. Heard it clear as an amen."

My grandmother said, "Jimmy was a good boy." As if he'd never grown up. "I'm sorry, Franklin."

I didn't know what to say, so I mumbled something about liking Jimmy Bee.

All the time that Jimmy Bee lay dying, Daddy must've been thinking on how to commemorate Jimmy's life when it was done. Because the morning after Jimmy's decease, Daddy was up to his elbows in plans—for a real Irish wake, to take place at the Bee residence. Jimmy was Irish and damn proud of it. Daddy started telephoning nonstop, dialing, talking, passing the news, till our phone line musta gotten pretty heated up. Miraculous Call agreed to be fiddler. That much I overheard. And just about everybody would contribute whiskey—nothing but Tennessee.

At the idea of a wake, my morbid side sparked to life. Forever, I'd been eager to view a cadaver—even if the body was Jimmy Bee. Right then, "The Mortifying Body Song" sang in my mind: *Your body turns a slimy green. The pus squirts out like shaving cream. The worms crawl in, the worms crawl out, the worms play pinochle on your snout.* At the wake I intended to study on Jimmy Bee's corpse so I could give Malcolm all the gory details.

Two days later, our town turned out to bid Jimmy Bee so long. There was Miss Grace Bando and Zora Brown and Harold Jasper and the Haggard clan and Russ Russell and Junior Junior Davis and Mrs. Purvis and Mr. Pruett. About everybody I knew. Two by two or in knots or by singles, people passed by our house, headed for the Bee place—some by automobile, a few on horseback, but most on foot—talking in a lively way as they went. As if it were a party, which is kind of what a wake is. Soon as Uncle Lucas arrived from Boston, I asked him about that, and he told me, "A wake's not a doleful thing. It's a boozy and jovial jubilation for a fallen friend."

From our front steps, I watched the parade pass. Most

of the people carried some sort of foodstuff. I saw hams and cakes and countless casseroles, gummy with Velveeta, go by—even a bowl of sloshing punch—transported by Jimmy's many friends.

I'd slicked back my hair with pomade and dressed in my best long pants and a gaudy green necktie, because Irish Jimmy Bee loved green. I wore a fresh white shirt. A starched one. Even though the collar itched my neck like all get-out, I was gonna put up with it. Jimmy Bee'd always been nice to me.

Lucas took one look at me and said gently, "Well now, ain't you just bedizened." *Bedizened.* It sounded like some kind of blessing, and I felt my slicked-up self glow.

My grandmother and Daddy and Lucas and I were halfway out the front door when Gold Ma began clanging her bell, like the outbreak of a four-alarm fire.

"Hold on," Daddy said. "I'll see to it." He was back in no time. "Gold Ma wants to go to the wake," Daddy told us. "She won't take no for an answer."

Her wheelchair was "incapacitated," to quote Daddy, so Gold Ma'd been housebound for some time.

While my daddy was talking, I could hear Gold Ma from upstairs. She was frail, but she wasn't too feeble to shout. "Franklin Lord Church!" she hollered. "You don't take me, I'll set a red-hot curse on you! I've known Jimmy Bee his en-tire life. Don't you dare leave me behind! Don't you—" Gold Ma coughed a spell, then railed on. "I'm goin' if I hafta walk! An' if that kills me, it's your fault and you're going straight to sulfuric hell!" I waited for Daddy to just stalk on out, allowing her to squawk herself to death.

"Mama," he said, "you and David wait here. Lucas and I'll be right back."

And they were. In about ten minutes' time, Daddy and Uncle Lucas returned—with as many of their cronies as they could round up. They all tromped into our house, pausing to remove their hats when they passed by my grandmother. "Mornin', Miz Church. Mornin', David." Then they kept right on slogging upstairs. I had an idea what they were up to, so I clumped right behind.

There began a great scuffle in Gold Ma's room. The cussed old woman'd already slid herself half out of bed and was nearly splayed out on the floor. So Daddy had to lift her back up and cover her chicken legs again. "I'm *goin'*," she kept saying. "Jes' try an' stop me!" She squawked like she was laying an egg, waggling her cane at Daddy's mob.

How one puny little soul could be so disruptive, I just had no idea.

"Dammit, we're not preventin' you," Daddy said with as much patience as he could muster. "We're *taking* you. All together now, boys. Heave 'er up!"

By then the cronies had encircled the four-poster bed. As in a weird dance, they crouched down and took ahold of the wooden bedstead, Gold Ma and all. I had a grip near her head, right close to all the screeching.

The bed began to rise, as if levitated. Not by spirits, but by real blood-and-bone men, who grunted and chuckled the while.

"Wait now!" Gold Ma suddenly ordered. So, slowly, we set the four-poster down.

Daddy asked, "What is it?"

"My bridge. Ain't goin' nowhere without it."

Daddy mumbled what surely was a curse. He picked up the water glass on her nightstand, crooked one finger, and fished a pinkish lump from the water—Gold Ma's dentures. She snatched them from Daddy and popped them between her wrinkly lips with a satisfying *click*. We all watched, mouths agape.

"Whatcha waitin' on?" Gold Ma asked peevishly.

We hoisted the bed again. Right off we hit an obstacle: no matter how we worked it, the bed wouldn't fit through the door frame. Well, it was an obstacle for only a breath or two. Then Daddy yelled, "Back up, ever'body, an' ram 'er on through!" Gold Ma gave a watered-down rebel yell as we gained speed. We all cheered when the bed struck and splintered up the jamb. Gold Ma barely bounced on impact, so we just kept right on going.

The bed caromed off the walls as we went, and by the time our crew'd maneuvered that hunk of furniture to the stairs landing, we were crying, limp with laughter. I was so overcome, I got the hiccups, which caused new waves of glee. To take the steps, we tilted the bed—and nearly chunked Gold Ma down the flight of stairs. She shrieked and we laughed louder. For support, Uncle Lucas grabbed ahold of the banister, convulsed so, for a minute he couldn't go on.

"You drop me," Gold Ma threatened, "I'll lay your skulls open!" Sounded like she was enjoying her moment.

Everybody guffawed. "Yes'm!" We kept wobbling our way to the bottom. There we set the bed down and sat ourselves down to recover. My grandmother looked at us sharply and said, "You-all drunk?"

"Why, no, Mama," Daddy said.

"No'm," Lucas backed him up, "but that's a hell of a good idea."

"Not a drop till you get Gold Ma to the Bees' house in safety."

Gold Ma announced, "*I'm* not lifting, I'll have a drink." Daddy fetched her a shot glass of Jack Daniel's Old No. 7.

"It'll kill her, Franklin," my grandmother mourned.

"She's too cantankerous to kill," said Daddy. "Okay, boys, Jimmy's waitin' on us. Let's git this show on the road." We lurched Gold Ma and her four-poster down the front steps and onto the sidewalk. We were about to heft her up for the last long stretch to the Bees' place when Gold Ma hollered, "Hold on!"

Down went the four-poster once more. "What in hell do you want now?" asked Daddy.

"Cut me some azaleas, David," Gold Ma said. "I'm taking them to Jimmy Bee."

What a wonder! You just never knew about a person. Gold Ma's mean as ten cats in a knot, but now she was sacrificing her prize flowers for Jimmy Bee. Maybe she felt guilty because she should have died before him. I went for the shears, clipped off the prettiest blooms I could find, and heaped them in Gold Ma's lap.

Then we bore her along in a giddy procession. Gold Ma perched up in bed, propped by pillows, gleaming in her black and yellow kimono, a lapful of bloodred azaleas and a well-satisfied look on her face. Passing pilgrims smiled. Or gaped. Or downright hooted. And they all saluted my great-grandmother, as, transported by her boisterous bearers, Gold Ma swooped up Cherokee Street, a wizened queen on her palanquin, headed for Jimmy Bee's wake.

I5.

While we grew up, Malcolm and I loved a lot of things with burning fire, one after the other. Our fickle hearts shifted like a gleam of trout, from stream to stream to stream. Once, Malcolm and I had entertained ourselves with the Brer Rabbit game. Another time, with our cave and cowboys and Indians and blood brothers. Once, with a sow hunt. Once, with the hope of viewing Jimmy Bee's corpse, though, unfortunately, at the wake the coffin'd been closed. But with time, these interests sputtered out. Apart from wanting to pay a visit to the morgue and longing to glimpse Charles Henry Bando's arm, playing baseball was the one thing that remained bright as a new dime. We believed we'd love the game of baseball forever. That was before summer came.

Malcolm and I had played baseball together ever since we'd met each other. We both owned baseballs and bats and gloves. We even shared a mouse, for better grip on the ball. That little rosin bag helped us pitch. Daddy'd bought it for me; he wanted me to be on top in everything. We'd fumbled catches and whiffled pitches—well, mostly I did. Once, Malcolm got smacked in the teeth when a grounder nicked a rut and jumped up. But those things were only hiccups on our road to success. We were going to be baseball players—professionals—the both of us. I'd be a doctor on the side.

The smell of my baseball glove was intoxicating. Sometimes I pressed my face into the pocket and breathed in. Then I was linked to all the champions, all the scrub players, all the boys who'd ever put on a glove or longed for one.

My hero was Harmon Killebrew, who'd played for the Chattanooga Lookouts. Malcolm's was "Hammerin' Hank" Aaron, who could clout homers and steal bases, slick as a greased snake.

Daddy was a fool for baseball. He listened to it on the radio and attended every game played within a few hours of our town, and most times he took me along. Despite the fact he wouldn't allow a colored person through his front door, despite the Nigger Rule, my daddy was also a fool for Jackie Robinson, who'd broken a barrier by being the first colored to play big-league ball. Hard as I tried, I could never get a grip on the man; Daddy slipped through my fingers like smoke—like the secret dark woman from his long-ago life.

Sometimes I wondered if Malcolm's daddy was as perplexing as mine. I only knew Mr. Deeter a little bit. The first time we met was at the post office. I was there mailing a letter to Uncle Lucas. (I didn't trust the mailbox outside our house not to lose my stuff.)

Malcolm and his daddy were there for stamps, Malcolm told me, on account of his daddy was a stamp collector. He often prowled the P.O. looking for new issues. The ones from Africa, Cameroon and such places, those were his favorites. He was a little, slight man. But right off, when I saw him, he reminded be of wire—thin but tough.

When Malcolm saw me he dragged his daddy over. "Hey, Daddy, this is—"

"Lemme guess," said Mr. Deeter. "You must be the David that Malcolm's always talkin' about. He finds you highly entertaining—more entertaining than his chores." His eyes sparked. Like Malcolm's. "Good to meet you, son."

He held out his hand; I gripped it.

"Hello, sir," I said.

Mr. Deeter didn't seem at all complicated. I believed he was the kind who'd invite me in to see his stamps; not a person who'd have a phantom stashed away somewhere or who'd set down an ugly rule—like Daddy.

Malcolm's daddy'd played ball with him since he was real little, shagging flies, retrieving grounders, showing him how to grip the bat. But Mr. Deeter didn't have to do much. Malcolm was a born ballplayer. For him, the game was like breathing. For me, it was a continual struggle. When I missed a ball, I'd pout like a baby, so bad did I want to play with Malcolm's ease. I'd blame my faults on anything around—the position of the sun, the slope of the ground, even the poor dumb trees.

"Damn glove!" I'd mutter sometimes, slamming it down.

"Hey, David. Watch."

Over time, Malcolm showed me how to better my play. He never strutted or got cocky. He never shamed me. Never.

White people and Negroes didn't play ball together. Not hardly. Not in our town. Not in Tennessee. But Daddy liked Jackie Robinson. So I devised a surefire scheme: Malcolm would become the junior Jackie Robinson. He'd be so good, so graceful, so fleet, so pantherine out in the field, nobody could deny him. Then, when Malcolm was successful beyond all dreams, maybe Daddy'd welcome him. Just *maybe* he could enter our home—without anybody shooting him.

"You outta your mind?" Malcolm said. "I can't try out for a white team." Malcolm knew how scary such a thing would be; he knew I was stark raving mad.

"'Course you can," I replied. "Can'tcha see the fans' faces? You'll be a hero. Like Jackie Robinson. There'll be no stoppin' you then."

"David, you're crazy as a cootie."

"You can come into my house then—see my room, meet Fats."

Despite his doubts, Malcolm got fixated on my idea.

To be the junior Jackie Robinson, that became his heart's desire. If only I'd known what would happen.

One day Malcolm and I'd stopped hitting fungoes and plopped on our bellies on the grass behind the white elementary school. Grasshoppers leaped in the weeds. A bird with russet wings perched on the nearby fence, making a little *tut-tut* sound. Then suddenly, it swooped down, snatched up a grasshopper, and swallowed it—legs, wings, and hop.

"Wonder how it feels to swallow a grasshopper," Malcolm said, his eyes glittering.

"Think I can live without knowin'."

"I can't."

Next thing I knew, he'd snatched one and gulped the damn thing down.

"Jesus H. Christ, Malcolm!" I yelled. Then I asked, "Is it wiggly?"

"Yeah."

My faith in Malcolm swelled. Now that he'd eaten a live grasshopper, I was sure he could do most anything. A boy who could play baseball and eat bugs. What more did you want in a friend?

To celebrate the bug swallowing, I found a dried-up grasshopper and took it home. That afternoon, I opened my trick box on the kitchen table. So far, I had about a dozen items hoarded up, from a worthless Confederate twenty to my prized Crimestoppers, tips on safety and how to nab criminals, little nuggets I'd clipped from the Sunday *Dick Tracy*s.

Grandmother was pouring hot paraffin on the currant jelly she was putting up, to seal it. "Keep your things from my paraffin, David," she said. "No grasshoppers in my jelly." Funny, though robbers lurked in the back of her mind, bugs didn't bother her. But, like me, surely she didn't want to *eat* them. While she was working and I was looking over my treasures, Daddy walked in.

"Whatcha got there, sonny boy?" he asked, pouring himself some iced tea from the pitcher on the table. *Christ A'mighty! The poem!* I jumped up and tried to scoop everything back into the trick box. "Just stuff," I mumbled, fumbling around.

"The Chink-box loot, eh? *Phoot!*" He made a sound like spitting. He reached out and snatched up the pebble that Mister Swann had stepped on. He grinned and flung it into the air, closer and closer to the ceiling fan. For a second I thought he was going to let the fan ricochet it so I'd never find it.

"Give it back," I said in a small swell of gumption.

"It'll cost you a dollar-three-eighty." Daddy thought he was funny.

Suddenly he drilled it at me.

"Catch, sonny."

I burned with fury.

"Real nice keepsakes," Daddy said in a voice that told me my treasures were foolish. But they weren't. They *weren't*.

Day after day, year after year, Malcolm and I pitched to each other and hit pop-ups till our arms felt limp as taffy. We honed our skills, waiting for the time we'd have the chance to play for the Panthers, the local squad. They were sponsored by Haggard's Drugstore.

The day came, sure enough. A day "hotter than a two-dollar pistol," to quote Uncle Lucas. Kids our age from all over town swarmed the field for tryouts. Nobody seemed to mind the heat. Nobody seemed to notice Malcolm. We figured they'd think he was working for Coach, till he asked for an opportunity to play. Everybody seemed intent on one thing only: making the team. Malcolm and I were ready, we thought. We were fired with hope.

The night before tryouts, I'd slept with a baseball under my pillow. Anything to enhance my chances. I was pretty nervous. When the big day dawned, I kept punching my fist into my glove.

"Hey." Malcolm grinned. "If glove thumping's rated, you're in like Flynn."

I gave him a sick smile. I looked around. Other kids were also punching their gloves.

"Dunno about that, I've got competition," I mumbled, because for added luck, I was working a plug of Bazooka in my mouth, like a wad of tobacco.

"You're a shoo-in, David."

"You, too. You gonna change the world."

"You think it's a good idea?" he asked. I could tell he was real jittery about walking up and trying out with white people.

"'Course," I said. "Ol' Jackie started just like this. Wait till they see you. They'll go pure-dee nuts."

The coach put us through our paces, pitching, hitting, fielding. Most of the parents were watching. They had to stand behind the fence and "to refrain from making any commentary." That meant not to advise their boys or hurrah them to sway the coach—or cuss if they messed up. My daddy arrived in his fedora, rooster-red tie, and white shirt. For baseball tryouts, I guess, the sleeves were rolled up.

"Luck, David." He waved a greeting. I was too tense to respond.

When some of us were on display, the rest tried to seem cool, calm, and energetic as hell. "Hey, batter, batter, batter," they droned the old chant.

Hey, butter, butter, butter, I said inside myself, trying like hell to keep calm.

The coach stalked the field among us, stone-faced. He didn't say much. Whenever I thought he was watching me, I got fluttery in my stomach, like I'd swallowed a field full of grasshoppers.

I swung at a pitch with my whole body, itching to smite its sweet spot and blast it past tomorrow. But my bat had other plans and took only a weak bite of the stitching. I heard Coach grunt. My head dropped like a sinker ball. I'd lost my chance for glory.

At last we gathered together on the lawn, most likely each boy spooling his own failings back through his mind like a picture-show reel. Every one of them looked sweaty and a little limp, probably with the same fear I felt—that I'd be cut. And, like me, somewhere in his heart, probably still clutching on to some slim splinter of hope.

The names were called. I'd clinched it. I was on the team. At first it didn't hit me. Then I think I whooped. In my worried world, I'd forgotten all about Malcolm. Now I looked everywhere for him. When I finally spotted him, I rushed up. "Hey, Malcolm! I made it!"

He just looked at me like a bird with the wings torn off.

"What's wrong?"

"Coach wouldn't let me try out. Told me, 'Git off this field, nigger.'"

"Huh?"

"It's *your* doing," Malcolm said, his lower lip trembling.

"But, Malcolm—"

"Niggers don't get to do what white boys can," he said. "You knew that."

"I didn't! Honest!" I shouted.

I wished Malcolm'd have butted me cranksided like Brer Rabbit did the Tar Baby. But he didn't. And he didn't cry. He just turned and walked away.

Suddenly, an image of Mister Swann lit my brain. He was dangling a dead mole by the tail. His eyes stared out from someplace beyond sorrow. His eyes were Malcolm's.

"It's a mistake!" I screamed, close on hysteria. I rushed up to the coach. My words skidded over each other. "Malcolm's better than me! Better than all of us put together! He's like Jackie Robinson! It's not fair! You gotta give him a chance. You gotta fix it!"

"No niggers on my squad," the coach said flatly. "Not even if he's John-the-hell-Henry."

The silence that followed was frightening. Our dreams were slipping away. Old shingles off a roof. All those folks. Not a one spoke up. Not a one seemed to see.

So. We'd fooled ourselves. Malcolm couldn't play. He wouldn't be the junior Jackie Robinson. I wanted the turf beneath my feet to yawn open and swallow me. I wanted to lie buried beneath the feet of ballplayers. But never again did I want to be one.

"I'm not playing," I whispered defiantly. I could feel tears warm my cheeks. I didn't try to hide them. I let them run.

I dropped my glove and started to stalk off.

"Pick it up," Daddy said.

"No."

"Pick it up."

I did. "I hate you," I said. "I do."

He slapped me. Then he tossed me a ball. "Catch."

Dull as a robot, I stuck out my glove. The ball fell into it like a dead star.

I played baseball as a Panther for one season only—as badly as I could. Then I got cut.

16.

Baseball was out of our lives. And I was out of Malcolm's. He blamed me for breaking his heart. I hadn't seen him since that day. I wanted to shrivel up. Malcolm was my best friend and I was his. Still, I might not see him again.

I couldn't think about anything else—not visiting the morgue, not doctoring, not the Reb arm. Sometimes my brain made me crazy, running around and around my questions. Was this the real reason Daddy'd tried to keep Malcolm and me apart? To spare our hearts from something terrible down the road? Something worse than not making a baseball squad? Or was it for the pure hatred of Negroes?

I decided it was the hatred. Daddy didn't focus much on hearts. "He was prob'ly in on it with Coach," I told myself, boiling mad with everything and everybody.

But sometimes I flipped things upside down. Then it was *my* fault Malcolm was gone. I had convinced him he could be like Jackie Robinson. Had I nudged him toward becoming another Mister Swann? I wanted to blot it out. I wanted to sleep and sleep in a deep pocket of the dark so I didn't have to think about any of it.

If I'd thought about it more, it might have occurred to

me that hanging around a white boy could get Malcolm in a world of trouble. Worse than being shamed in front of some kids and their folks. But that idea didn't flicker into my mind. Not then. Not even with the Nigger Rule staring me down.

Sometimes, when I thought about Malcolm, I whispered a small and selfish prayer to Somewhere: "Let him come back, oh, please let him."

It wasn't my prayers that brought Malcolm. In a roundabout way, it was Charles Henry Bando's arm.

That dried-up Confederate limb had been forever niggling at our minds, Malcolm's and mine. So we'd always been real nice to Miss Grace, offering our services for all sorts of chores. And we'd been real brazen, not a bit ashamed. We just watched out in case she got suspicious.

Malcolm operated on a certain philosophy about working for Miss Grace: No matter how things turned out, we didn't lose a thing. At the very least, we made money, and if we were lucky, we'd get to see the arm.

I'd been washing Miss Grace's windows one day. I soaped them good, rinsed them with a garden hose, then dried them, enjoying the small squeaks rubbed up by the chamois I was using. Miss Grace with her kindly ways never expected perfection, so it should've been kinda fun. But the whole time I was working, I kept hearing Daddy's menacing voice: "Do it again, sonny boy. Do it again."

To distract myself, I thought about what Malcolm might be doing. He was probably on an errand for his folks, downtown. I imagined him going along, swinging the dumb-ass little black parasol he always carried—since his first confrontation with Hell. Ever after that Halloween squabble, Malcolm cut a wide swath around that old rooster. He'd go clear to the other side of the street, armed with his grandmother's little collapsible umbrella. To my mind, he might as well have used a fly swatter for defense.

The parasol was itty-bitty and frilly. "You should brandish a sword," I told him once, "a knife at the very least."

"Parasol suits me dandy," he said. He didn't give a hoot if he looked silly as all get-out. He was armed. He was safe.

Time to time, instead of scrubbing the window glass, I found myself frozen—thinking of Malcolm.

By the I time I'd finished, evening was coming on. The first stars pricked the sky.

"Why, thank you, David," Miss Grace said when the job was done. "I plan on recommending you to our entire town. Those windows sparkle just like Solomon's diamonds."

"Thank you, ma'am."

Though she paid me a sizable amount, and in Liberty half-dollars, the job was disappointing from my standpoint. I'd poked around as much as I could without getting caught, but I'd never glimpsed so much as a pinkie nail that didn't belong to a living person. My opinion of Miss Grace Bando jumped several notches every time I nosed around her house. She had that arm ensconced in a real good place.

I walked back home, chinking the coins in my pocket. They made a comforting sound. On the sidewalk lay withered magnolia blossoms, curled and brown like small cigars. I picked one up and pretended to puff on it and knock off the ashes, like a huffy ol' banker. The dark petal still smelled lemony.

Suddenly, I heard a commotion. Voices hooting and hollering. And raw laughter, punctuated with screams and crazy squawking. I could hear the *whup* of wings, flapping like a paper fan. *"No!"* I was already running.

A crowd of men was clotted around Malcolm, goading ol' Hell to peck him. Somebody—Jude Haggard, I think—was holding Malcolm so he couldn't run. Little weeps of blood had formed where Hell's beak had rent his pant legs. I remember the red. Though he wore a beat-up hat, that damn Slur Tucker, primed with drink, was twirling Malcolm's umbrella above his head.

"Lawsy," he taunted Malcolm, all slurry, mimicking Negro speech and flouncing around, "thas sun do burn! Looky here, it done tur' me *buh-lack*!" He hiccupped an ugly laugh.

Malcolm was hollering and crying and wriggling,

trying to twist out of Hell's way, but that damn rooster kept coming at him. Malcolm was sobbing, but nobody moved to help him. Still on the run, I plunged right into the midst of them, my fists lashing every which way, screaming, "Quit it! Leave him be!"

I stood between Malcolm and that feathered devil—and the rest of them—panting. I was so scared I could feel my blood throbbing. Then, in his blind flur of twists, Malcolm flailed the hat from Slur's head. Slur began spewing blasphemies, lurching for Malcolm, snatching air. Jesus God! Now Malcolm's worse than dead, I thought. The men moved back. Malcolm grabbed my shoulder, gulping sobs. He clutched me so tight, his tears ran down my neck.

"Run, Malcolm! Run!"

He looked at me, his eyes blank. Then he tore outta there.

"You *betta* run, niggah!" Slur Tucker reeled and yelled, falling-down-knee-walkin' drunk. "Slappin' off mah hat— Klan'll be comin' fo' ya! Klan gonna catch up to yore sorry black ass!"

I moaned. A hat. People had been killed over less.

It got real silent. Like when the organ in church stops to take a breath. Somebody gathered up Hell and set a croker sack over his head to shut him up. I don't recall who it was, I was so aflame with anger. When I finally focused on those men, I saw Daddy.

He had an odd look on his face. Something I couldn't read, but it was not shame. I clenched my fists. Words chanted inside me: *Please, don't make me be like him. Please, don't make me be like him.*

I needn't have worried. I guess I took after Lucas, 'cause I never could accept Daddy's way. We were like two people tugging in different directions on the same rope.

When I reached home, I ran to my room, slammed the door, and cried till I had no tears left. I got up slowly and opened my trick box. I read the poem hidden there to myself:

Malcolm. He's my brother.
His eyes spark like the devil.
He can piss a whole lot
farther than me.
And he knows the bone names.
I love him.

I took a pencil and scrawled over the last line, bigger and darker.

My brother. He was in danger.

I didn't go down to supper. Sometime late a rap came; then Daddy walked in. "Lord, David," he said, "it was just a joke." I looked away from him, out the window. Silence stole in and chilled the room. I sat stiff as a corpse. Daddy must have known I wouldn't talk, not even if he knocked the sap out of me, so without another word, he went out. I kept on staring into the night. I could feel the dark.

17.

I dreamed that somebody had come back to life. Got back the breath that had once lifted his lungs. Got back his blood, his very light.

It was Sunday and I was leaving church. Outside, a man was waiting for me. Not flashy. Not fine. Just a man.

"David," he said.

Everybody else floated off. He looked into my eyes and he knew me, clear through. I was unafraid. I knew him, too. I had always wondered.

"Fats."

"Come back to greet you, with my flesh on." He grinned like a sunbeam.

"You look real good."

We linked arms and walked out into the sun. Right down Main Street we strolled, arm in arm, as one.

"How do you spell 'rat'?" I asked him, applying our family test to know something of the man he'd been. He'd hung around long enough to know the response.

He answered directly.

"R-a-t, as in 'rat now.'" Fats had humor; he'd do.

"You've taught me things," I said.

"Yeah?"

"Shoot, yeah. All about the human bones."

"Glad o' that. But I'm here now 'bout the human heart."

I waited.

"Love," he said in a sweet song-voice.

"What?"

"Love." His voice rang all around us, beautiful as a hymn. It shimmered in the leaves of the trees. And along the pavement. Till my bones sang with it.

He began to rise slightly. Our arms tugged, then unlinked as, in a radiance, he lifted, high and higher.

"Wait!"

"Love!"

"How'd you—"

"*Love!*" He near drowned me out.

"—die?"

From beyond the clouds, he called down to me.

"Lynched."

18.

The morning after Hell's attack, I, wooden-boy, shuffled into the kitchen to help my grandmother fix breakfast. She had called me, I had come. When I entered the room, she was sweeping up imaginary crumbs, the broom whispering over the linoleum. I was still boiling about Malcolm. The only words I had left were *yes'm* and *no'm*.

Suddenly, the doorbell rang, sparing me a scolding over my deportment.

"Go see who that is, will you, David?"

I did. On the way, I passed Daddy. He was sitting in his armchair reading his precious *News Free-Press*. But he did not look up.

I peeped through the screen door. A woman I'd never laid eyes on before was standing there. She was big boned, but not heavy. She wore a flowered dress and a straw hat with a spill of fake roses over the brim. Her shoes looked soft and old—like they knew a road or two—and her skin was the color of polished licorice, the darkest I'd ever seen. There was something about her, frightening and soft at once—a sibyl from Bible times come to life. From pictures I'd seen of Michelangelo's chapel, I knew a sibyl right off.

The woman smelled of talcum and righteousness, a fearful combination.

"Hello, David, I'm Tinney. Up from Howard." Howard was the Negro section, down near the outskirts of town. I was so amazed to hear my name, my words stuck.

Before I could think of a one, Daddy was there. He opened the screen door, walked her inside, and embraced her. At least he tried to, but the woman rebuffed him. She looked at Daddy like she longed to snap him in two. The shock near sucked the breath from me.

Who was this dark woman who knew my name? Why in God's world had Daddy allowed her in? *Touched her!* I was utterly confounded. I simply couldn't solve it—the puzzle that was my daddy.

I must have just stood there gaping like a jackass.

"Go on, David," Daddy said. "Tinney and I gonna talk."

And they did. For a long time. I sat on the stairs and gathered snatches of their words, murmuring, rising, slapping at each other like the varied voices of water. Hers, in particular, stormed. I leaned my whole body into listening but could catch only angry scraps, the gist being "Leave Malcolm Deeter be." I began to clench my fists nervously. Any second now Daddy was gonna grab hold of his shotgun and blast that old woman to Kingdom Come.

No blast came. After a time, Daddy ushered Tinney to the front door again. From where I sat, I could see her plainly. Her eyes blazed white against her skin. They softened then. She was looking at me.

"David," she said, "come on over here." When she opened her mouth this time, I noticed that she hadn't a tooth in her head. But she was chewing a cud of gum, Juicy Fruit, from the aroma. Making smoochy little sounds. I instantly revered her.

I hopped up and went right quick. The mysterious Tinney slowly leaned down. Her dress seemed like an entire field of flowers.

"I been watchin' you since the day you were born."

Her voice was warm. I was stunned. I drew in a breath and tried to understand this unsettling thing: a stranger had been following my growth my entire eleven years.

"Thank you," I said, then felt foolish. You don't thank somebody for caring about you. But why did she? And what Negro held such sway over my daddy, she could just waltz through our front door and give him hell?

My mind sparked. Was this Daddy's phantom? The long-lost woman I'd heard of time to time? The main thing was, she loved Malcolm. Maybe she'd see he was kept from harm.

How *was* Malcolm? Were those Hell-pecks okay? Sure. They'd probably heal up in a couple of days. But what if Slur Tucker wasn't just ranting? He was a hater. Though Malcolm had accidentally swatted his hat, it was all Slur

Tucker needed to go after him. It made me sick, thinking about that.

When Tinney was gone, I went into the parlor. I had to ask my daddy something. I felt real jittery. He'd been reasonable just now with Tinney, but he could shift easy as a kite in wind. He could turn mean. Which Daddy would he be with me?

"Daddy, who's Tinney?"

His eyes never left his newspaper. He just said, "Never you mind."

Not long after Tinney's visit, Malcolm slipped out to see me. He seemed jumpy and kept looking around. We were hunkered in the shadow of a big pecan, talking low about some fool thing. Suddenly, I knew somebody was watching us. I felt it. Before I could holler *"Look out! Slur Tucker!"* from nowhere a figure sprang at Malcolm. Like a bear trap, he clamped onto one arm and rasped, "Git on home!" Then he firmly escorted Malcolm toward Howard.

Mr. Deeter! I nearly keeled with relief. Well now. Maybe I was wrong about him inviting me into their home; by now, maybe Mr. Deeter had set down a rule of his own: Don't fraternize with that white boy or I'll gut him like a bass. The White-Boy Rule. Bless Jesus! Wouldn't Daddy just turn blue!

19.

The rest of that year drifted off like haze, and another came, 1954.

Rue Lynne Haggard was getting married. Homely as hog jowls, my daddy called her. But she was rich, being the daughter of Jude Haggard. The family lived over on Oak Street, in a big white house with tall white columns, like in plantation days. It had a huge space out back, more like a field than a yard. That's where the wedding reception took place. The cars and trucks were clotted together, parked beyond the party grounds.

Grandmother had arranged with Lily to stay with Gold Ma, to tend to her needs and maybe help her work on one of her afghans, "the ugliest goddamn things in creation," to Daddy's way of thinking.

I'd washed the Buick for the occasion. This time it had passed the Daddy Test right off, and now it gleamed like a big black bullet. Daddy drove puffed up behind the wheel, like he was the king of Spain.

During the wedding supper, Rue Lynne's daddy gave a toast. He lifted his glass of champagne. "Rue Lynne's marryin'," Jude Haggard roared heartily. "Damn well time. Tom Davis is gettin' my Rue Lynne," he joked, "along with a whole string o' camels. An' hogs. An' goats. Jes' like in Arabia." As if he were giving whatever was needed to be rid of his daughter. Jude thought that was pretty funny. So did most of the guests.

I thought it was stupid. Shoot, who cared if she was married or not? Didn't make her any better off than she already was. I guess Rue Lynne cared. The livestock joke didn't appear to affect her in the least. She looked triumphant. Like a cat who'd swallowed a bird, chirp and all.

The wedding gifts were displayed alongside the tables where we were eating, so the guests could oogle them. I went to oogle them myself. Real fancy linens and glasses that looked like they'd been gouged up in knife fights. And an egg slicer, for cripessake! And some dumb stuff I didn't even recognize. Mostly there were a whole lot of toasters. How could so many people hit on the same gift? I wondered. Everybody around here must live on toast.

Right smack during supper, Rue Lynne, scented with enough lilac to lay you out cold for a week, hopped onto a table. She'd been slurping champagne from the beginning. The way she wobbled in her high heels, you could tell she was beyond tipsy.

"Hey!" she shrieked. "We're top-heavy on toasters. You gonna do somethin' 'bout it?"

"Hell, yes!" came a slurred chorus.

Immediately most of the men and some of the women

sprang for their guns—always at the ready in their vehicles—leaving their suppers to go cold. Daddy was about the first one gone. I didn't mind. Shooting toasters was a far cry from cats. Still, it was about the jackassest thing I ever did hear of.

The help lined up the toasters down at one end of the lawn. Rue Lynne snapped her garter into the air and hollered, "Go!" The Great Toaster Shoot was on. Too bad Malcolm was missing it. This was the kind of thing that bloomed into his most gorgeous stories.

"You-all stop it!" Viyella Smith hollered, vexed as all get-out when somebody took aim at her gift. "I paid good money for that!"

Orville Potter, nicknamed Open-Another-Bottle, shushed her. "Hush up, you ol' poop, an' enjoy the shoot."

The shooters took turns. Jude Haggard kept score, except for when he was a participant. Since toasters don't move of their own accord, it should have been like shooting fish in a barrel. Except that the shooters moved a lot—soused to the last one and acting like they'd been dumped on their heads at birth.

"Got me a GE!" somebody hooted when he hit a target.

"Westinghouse! *Bull's-eye!*" whooped somebody else. They missed more than they struck pay dirt, sometimes winging an oak or a black walnut tree, laughing so hard the tears coursed down their cheeks in runnels. The raucous guests squealed encouragement right along, ducking to avoid ricochets.

Rue Lynne and Tom enjoyed the Shoot as much as anybody. They took pot shots at the appliances before the event was called to a halt on account of a lack of ammunition.

Daddy rarely drank spirits, except on holidays. This day he did. In spite of that, he shot like he was touched by the hand of God. He hit nearly every toaster set before him. For his impressive marksmanship, he won a pair of Tappan two-slicers, banged up as hell. He was showing off his trophies, carrying on like a fool. I wanted to see, so I went to where most everybody was milling around out back.

"Whatcha gonna do with them damn things, Franklin?" Miraculous Call asked.

"Somethin'," he replied sloppily. Then, lugging one under each arm to the Buick, my daddy added, "Too bad they ain't niggers."

The words hit me like a fist. I sneaked on back to the party before Daddy could see me.

The shooters were hauling off the toasters like wounded Confederates. "Gee," Rue Lynne said, all weepy, "there's not a one left for me. I cain't cook. With no toast, what'll we *eat*?"

"Don' you worry, honey." Daddy winked at her and chuckled. "Soon's I get home, I'll sen' you a bran' spankin' new un."

Daddy slumped into our automobile, where my grandmother and I were already waiting. He nearly flooded the engine, but after a few attempts and a good pounding to the dashboard, Daddy got it to kick over and started out the drive.

He fumbled with the gears till they squealed. "Damn Sam!" he swore. "Where the hell's reverse gone to?" He crunched the gears again. The Buick bucked, then Daddy was backing up, doing okay till he struck a power pole. A good jolt. Daddy charged the pole again. *Rrrrr.*

Though we were nearly at a standstill, Grandmother Church spoke up nervously. "Please, Franklin," she said in a trembly voice, "watch what you're doing. You'll get us all killed."

Daddy turned around and shot her a hard look.

"*You* wanna drive, Mama?"

She didn't know how.

"No, Franklin."

Kaleidoscope click. I realized something. My grandmother was afraid of Daddy.

Nobody spoke after that. Daddy lurched from the car, kicked the whitewalls a coupla times, and shouted, "Behave yo'self, no-account damn fool hunk o' junk!" Then he sagged back in, gunned the Buick, and somehow drove it home. I guess it knew the way.

First thing Daddy did, he lugged his battered toasters

into the parlor. He swiped some of Grandmother's books from the shelves and onto the floor, to stuff his trophies in. "Booken's," he mumbled, grinning the whole time, "right smart booken's."

"David," my grandmother said softly.

"Yes'm?"

"Take some wedding cake up to Gold Ma, will you?" She served a slice on one of Gold Ma's best plates, from her wedding. It had dainty blue flowers painted on it.

Then she said goodnight to me and went to her room. She was crying.

When I went in, I set the cake plate down on Gold Ma's nightstand, then folded up the afghan she'd been working on. Lily'd already gone.

"What's that?" Gold Ma asked, eyeing the cake and sniffing at it like a mouse.

"Wedding cake. Rue Lynne Haggard got married." It was a big hunk, so I cut her off a wedge.

"To who? That Beale boy?"

"Uh-uh. Tom Davis."

Gold Ma snorted. "She'll regret it right quick. He's a rapscallion, that one." I didn't mention that Rue Lynne was a rapscallion, too.

Gold Ma stuck her skinny fingers into the cake and ate some, smearing icing on her chin. Crumbs stuck to her lips. Even after they were licked clean, she kept on licking, working her wet lips greedily.

I was taking the leftovers out when Gold Ma stopped me. "Your nigra friend's not getting any o' that cake," she announced.

If the day had been different, I'd have let those words roll. But after Daddy's talk in the car park, they were more than I could bear. I didn't give a rat's ass what I said. I grabbed for the thing most hateful to her.

"*You're* a nigra!" It shot out like an *abracadabra* that could instantly turn her skin dark. "You're a nigra and you can't stand it, so you hate every one of them!"

Gold Ma looked like she was about to disintegrate. She lunged at me and threw her call bell. But she was weak and it just thudded to the floor, a dud grenade. She threw everything she could get ahold of, shrieking and cussing. A deranged witch. "You little sum-bitch! Damn you to hell! Damn your little ape friend! I curse you to your bones, David Church! I disown you! Franklin! Frank-*lin*!"

Spittle dribbled down the sides of her mouth. Her crazed eyes burned like coals. I've never seen anybody so mad. The hate fit left her gasping.

The door banged open.

"Wha' the hell's goin' on?" Daddy shouted, still drunk. I stood there trembling.

"Yore bastard boy called me nigra!" hissed Gold Ma.

The room went deadly silent. I could feel my life pump through my veins.

"That right?" Daddy's face was stiff like it was shellacked.

"Yessir."

Suddenly, Daddy snapped me up by my shirt collar, a savage look in his eyes. "'Pologize," he snarled real low. "You 'pologize now or so he'p me God . . ." He was choking me.

I hesitated.

"Say it!" The veins bulged in his neck.

"I'm sor-ry, G-Gold M-Ma," I strangled out.

Before I could think, Daddy dragged me to my room. He was going to wear me out, sure. But he didn't. Instead, he snatched up my trick box. "You an' Lucas an' your Chinks an' your niggers!" he raged. "An' that damn Malcolm Deeter. You better keep clear o' him, boy. This ain't kid stuff no more." The threat struck the air like the clap of a broken bell. Then Daddy frog-marched me down the stairs.

"You're hurting me," I rasped.

"Damn right I am."

"Franklin, don't!" A frightened voice was whimpering, adding to the din. My grandmother, cowering at the bottom of the stairs. But Daddy didn't stop—or even notice her, I don't think. He hauled me out back.

"I'll teach you yore manners, boy. I'll teach you a less'n you'll never fergit." He let go of me and I gripped my throat and retched into the bushes.

"See this?" he asked, shoving the trick box in my face.

"Ye-s-s-ir."

"Well, tell it g'bye, sonny boy." First he hacked it to pieces with the ancient ax. Then he hurled the splinters into the privy. With all his might. Down into the shit.

20.

After the destruction of my treasures, I wrapped myself in anger like a thick winter coat. I never set foot in Gold Ma's room, except when I couldn't avoid it. Those times, I crossed my fingers when I entered. Crossing your fingers *x*-es things out.

Malcolm and I barely saw each other. Though Slur Tucker's threat had come a time back, hereabouts grudges burrowed deep, like ticks. But, in spite of his fears for his life, and his folks' watchfulness, Malcolm wasn't the kind to be pushed. He ghosted around our street. I felt it. He was real elusive, too smart to get caught again, but I kept an eye out. First chance I got, I told him what Daddy'd done—and said.

"Guess I best lay low a speck longer. Like Brer Rabbit." There was no humor behind Malcolm's words. Just defiance. "So long."

My grandmother was a reader. She had a book called *Sequoyah* and she shared it with me. At first, I thought she wanted me to learn about those big ol' California trees. Nope. She wanted me to know of a Cherokee man she admired. By the time I finished that book, he was my hero, too.

That Sequoyah. Most of his life he was nobody, just a crippled man from Tennessee who worked metal into spoons and forks and such. And who loved his Cherokee people. They had no written language. Sequoyah knew without one, their voices would be forever lost. So, though he couldn't even read, he invented a way for those people to write.

That sure was something! If ol' Sequoyah could do it, I could, too. For a time after that, nights, I forgot about bones and noodled at my desk, devising a code. It was a struggle. But when at last I wrote my weird symbols beside English letters, I smiled. I had myself a secret language.

One time, real secretive-like, I handed the sheet of symbols to Malcolm. He looked it over. "I made up a language," I said. "We can write—"

"And nobody'll know what we're saying." Malcolm grinned. So we scrawled messages on little scraps of paper and hid them in a dozen locations all over town. We didn't lose each other.

At last, Christmas came. The holiday that arrives as softly as snow whitening the land, turning even ugly things beautiful.

Snow is a rare thing in our part of Tennessee, but that year it fell. Just a dusting—to let you know God was still watching.

In our house, Christmas was a time of ironing. Along with the scent of pine from our tree, a warm singe-y smell filled the air. Lily focused on the sheets, in case we had visitors, and in particular on the Christmas linens. She arranged herself in a slat-back chair in the sewing room before a contraption called a mangle. To operate it, you fed the item you wanted pressed through one end of its hot metal jaws. It poured out at the other side.

I liked to watch Lily at work. In a quiet rhythm, she would ease a wrinkled sheet through the tight-lipped mangle. Slowly, it billowed out again, voluminous and white. Like the wings of an angel.

Christmas was also a time of baking. Beginning in November, our life moved into the kitchen, where my grandmother and I tackled fruitcakes and plum puddings and cookies—whatever we could prepare ahead—with zeal. We fixed lemon snowballs and Ruta's thumbprint cookies and butter cookies sprinkled with nonpareils, which caught in the grouting each year and stayed there forever. Whenever my grandmother made Gold Ma's favorites, oozy with jelly, I weaseled out of it. We made whiskey balls by the tin. At whiskey-ball time, Daddy and Uncle Lucas, if he decided to come, tested them—and the whiskey—and got tight. And argued a lot.

Sure enough, one evening close to Christmas, I heard a scuffling on the screened porch. I peeked out. My heart jumped. Uncle Lucas! He'd slung a big lumpy bag over his shoulder, so he looked like Santy Claus. All he needed was a red suit and cap and a bushy white beard. I longed to get a chance to peep inside that bag, to see what he'd brought me. But I didn't hold out much hope of that. Lucas was a wily one. He could hide things even better than Miss Grace.

Once he'd shed the sack in some tricky place, Uncle Lucas headed straight for the kitchen, sniffing like a hound. As he lumbered along he bayed "That's What I Like about the South," a song about Doo-wah-diddy, an itty-bitty speck of a Southern place. Awful pretty, awful nice. Lucas belted it out like you would the national anthem. But I got a feeling—he might've missed the South, but he didn't like it much.

"Whatcha cookin', Mama?" he asked, plunging a finger into the saucepan full of gravy my grandmother was stirring on a front burner of the cookstove.

"Lucas!" she greeted him with a timid whack of a spoon to the knuckles. "Don't you go poking your filthy fingers into my supper." Then she hugged him. And she cried. He boomed out a laugh and took another lick.

After he'd settled in, Uncle Lucas went back to the kitchen and put on one of my grandmother's aprons, three or four sizes too small. He stood in the middle of the cooking frenzy and stuck out his belly far as he could. A bovine

in a lace midriff. He washed his hands at the pump next
to the sink. "Gimme a job, Mama," he said. Grandmother
Church took one look at him and smiled—and cried all
over again. When she'd recovered, my grandmother
allowed Uncle Lucas to hull walnut meats—out on the
porch so she'd have some elbow room.

I could hear him out there shuffling the walnuts in a
tub, popping their skulls open in small explosions—*ca-rack!*
ca-rack!—serenading whoever'd listen about cigareetes 'n'
whiskey 'n' wile, wile women.

I went out there, too. For a long time, I'd been bottling
up a question. Daddy wouldn't answer it, so it must be a
secret. I never tried my grandmother, for fear she'd just
keel. I looked to see if anybody else was within earshot.

"Who's Tinney?" I blurted.

"Just why's this poppin' up outta the wile blue yonder?"

"She came by a while back. Daddy let her in—through
the front door."

"Well, David, it's no family skeleton. She's blood kin
to your friend Malcolm. Tinney Wilkes was your daddy's
mammy."

I felt my jaw flap open. "You mean she raised
Daddy?"

"Like he was her natural baby."

Even though he had a mama, most every baby had a
mammy, too, at least in Daddy's time. I knew that. Still, I

just gaped like an ape. "Raised me, too, sugar. But yore daddy, he was her pet. Franklin loves Tinney Wilkes like his very own mama."

I couldn't believe it. I learned right then, some love is absolute. Too potent to be poisoned, by Gold Ma or anybody. Tinney's love had taken hold a long time ago. It was a powerful thing—enough to make Daddy color-blind, leastways toward Tinney.

21.

The day before Christmas, Miss Grace sent for us through her faithful Zora. Malcolm and I were to hurry on over there on account of she needed immediate help. Malcolm was the invisible man, so I left him word, in code.

Things sounded like Miss Grace was in a real fix. Grandmother Church needed me, too, of course, for a thousand and two different chores. Still, Miss Grace and that ol' cutoff stump gave a more powerful tug. I dipped out of the house soon as I could and raced to her place. Malcolm was already there. I could just make him out, sitting in the shadows of the camellias by her steps like a mouser poised to pounce. Johnny-at-the-rathole, Lucas would have called him.

"What took you so long?" Malcolm said as if we saw each other every day, like before.

"Escaping my grandmother's like fleeing the pen. Let's get a move on. Her bloodhounds'll be snuffling me down right soon."

For a little bit we buzzed like wasps, catching up on what we'd missed of each other's doings. But mainly we were in a fret to start the job.

We rapped at the door. Presently, Miss Grace opened it. "Boys!" she greeted us. "Bless you-all's hearts for coming."

"More sow trouble?" I asked, hopeful of earning another dollar.

"Not hardly. Mercifully, Geth is right here on the premises." While she spoke, I scanned around. You never knew. You could get lucky and spot that arm. "Truth be told, boys, I'm up to my eyeballs in linen troubles."

I was mystified. And concerned. "You mean—you want us to *press* some things?"

"Lord, no!" Miss Grace laughed like tinkling glass. "David, you just tickle me to death, you are such a humorous young man. I need you-all to help clean out my linen closet. My eyes must be going. I simply cannot find my Christmas things. Without Christmas linens, how can anybody possibly celebrate the holiday properly?"

I'd never thought about that, so I had no ready reply. Neither did Malcolm.

In a rustle of black crepe, Miss Grace ushered us to her linen closet. We'd never set foot upstairs before, so my eyes patrolled the new territory the whole time, till I thought they might give out like catfish eggs in the sun.

"Here we are, boys," Miss Grace said. "Dive in."

To reach the shelves, I stood on tippy-toe on a chair and handed down the linens to Malcolm. They smelled of starch and mothballs and pomander, with just a hint of mildew, or feet. He set them in stacks on the floor, taking care not to topple them. There were piles of towels and washcloths and crocheted doilies and antimacassars and plain napkins and plain tablecloths and fancy napkins and fancy tablecloths of varied colors. None seemed to be what she was after.

"What're we looking for?" I asked.

"A big white cloth, stenciled with red and green swags and pine boughs," said Miss Grace. "My mama, God rest her soul, did the stencilwork herself. You'll know it right off."

The closet was dark and deep. I kept hauling things out to no avail. Suddenly, "What the devil—" I gave a holler and jumped back and fell off the chair.

"Well, I swan," said Miss Grace, "what in God's name's come over you, David Church? You see a rat?"

"A *arm!*" I scrambled back up. Then, with a flourish, I swung the trophy into view.

In one shining moment our lifetime ambition was achieved. I was holding the legendary item! Long as a good-size trout, with nails like claws, and hairier than I'd ever imagined a Confederate arm to be. The hand was in good shape. Clearly, no varmint had as yet discovered it. The color was hard to describe. The closest I could come was the shade of an ancient baseball. The wrinkly skin looked to be tough as baseball hide, too. 'Course, only the hand and wrist were visible, the arm itself being encased in a moth-eaten gray sleeve of Rebel origin.

That moment was the high point of my life thus far. I was about to bust. I couldn't wait to tell Uncle Lucas.

"Oh, *that*," said Miss Grace. "It's my great-granddaddy's. Charles Henry Bando and the limb became separated in battle." Her eyes looked so mirthful, you could've taken her for one of Santy's elves.

"Well, I'll be damned," said Malcolm, forgetting his manners. "What's it doin' here?"

"Where does your grandmother keep arms?" asked Miss Grace. "I classify it as linens, on account o' the sleeve. It's wool, you know."

Finally, Malcolm croaked out, "Can *I* touch it?"

"You surely may. By now Great-Granddaddy's dust. He's in no condition to object."

Malcolm and I passed the arm back and forth, like it was a holy relic.

"You want it?" Miss Grace asked. I nearly swooned. "I've got no kin. When my time comes, I'll see that you boys inherit it—if you'd so desire."

If we'd so desire! Jeez! I was way past flabbergasted.

"We want it," I said. "Don't we, Malcolm?"

"An' *how!*"

How do you thank somebody who's bequeathed you such a treasure? I settled on a formal, "Thank you a lot, Miz Bando."

Though we didn't actually receive the arm right then,

I felt as though we had. Forgetting our fears about Slur Tucker and Daddy, Malcolm and I whooped and hooted and cavorted down Cherokee Street, raucous as crows, delivered for the moment from all evil. Many Christmases have come and gone since then, but I was never given a more wonderful gift than that stuffed Confederate arm.

That old alligator. Miss Grace never mentioned her Christmas things again. I suspected she'd set us up. She'd known we were after her heirloom right along.

It was Christmas Day. Four o'clock in the afternoon. My family was seated at the dining table, Grandmother and Daddy and Uncle Lucas and me, even shriveled old Gold Ma. She was tied into her wheelchair, now back in business, with a wide red ribbon, as though somebody were receiving a mummy for Christmas. Of course, looking like a mummy didn't dull her tongue any. On account of our difficulties, I sat by the sideboard, as far away from her as I could—and close to the food.

"Who's that interloper down there?" Gold Ma squinted. "That the bastard?" The old witch damn well knew who it was.

"That's enough, Gold Ma. It's Christmas," said Uncle Lucas. Anger flared in his voice. "And that's David."

"The bastard," she repeated. I didn't give her the satisfaction of looking up.

Christmas dinner with all the trimmings steamed before

us in aromatic abundance. My greedy eyes took it in: roast turkey with pecan dressing, pork loin with mustard sauce, green apples sautéed in brandy that Uncle Lucas had brought from France, baby sweet corn we'd put up last summer, garden-grown beans, spoon bread with black-berry preserves, milk gravy galore, and Gold Ma's famous dumplings. When I served myself, though I dearly wanted some, I avoided those dumplings like the smallpox. On the sideboard the desserts were arrayed, the sweetest army, including my favorite, devil's food layer cake, heavy as lead. And there was a cut-glass bowl of glossy ribbon candy. And another with chunks of velvet-brown fudge and creamy-white hunks of divinity. There was also a brimming bowl of eggnog laced with whiskey. "To grow hair on your chest," said Uncle Lucas. In my view, it could have grown hair on your whole body.

We'd come to the table not to eat of this plenitude, but to gorge. Before we dove in, Daddy gave the blessing. "Thank you, Lord, for this bounty. And for this family. Let love abide among men. In Jesus's name. Amen."

My mind darkened. Yeah, I thought. Let love abide. Does that mean setting roosters on children? Choking boys and smashing their hearts to smithereens? I tried to scald him with my eyes.

The feasting began.

"'Save the bones for Henry Jones 'cause he don' eat no

meat!'" Uncle Lucas intoned. He smacked his belly with his meaty hands. "David, notice where I place my chair?" he said, eyes agleam over his heaping plate. I looked. "Six inches from the table. Know why?"

"Now, Lucas," Grandmother Church cautioned him quietly, "you be a gentleman." She knew what was coming.

"Aren't I always, Mama?" He twinkled. "Know why, David?" he pressed on.

Sure I did. He went through this same performance at every family feast. "Why, Uncle Lucas?" I asked anyway. That was my job.

"'Cause when my belly meets the wood, I know I'm done." He roared raucously and thumped his paunch again. Uncle Lucas began eating with gusto. When he chewed, his beard wigwagged up and down.

I slid my chair back from the table, just an inch. Then I began shoveling down my dinner, eager to finish and get to the presents. I gorged myself into a stupor, working on my belly meeting wood.

In the middle of dinner, the doorbell rang.

"Who the hell can that be?" said Daddy, getting up from the table. Christmas didn't stop him from cussing.

"What'd ya want?" I heard him ask somebody.

"Trap you a mole this afternoon?" said a high, thin voice. "In return for a speck o' food?" The soft words floated through the open door, into the dining room. Suddenly, I felt sick.

"For Chrissake," snarled Daddy. "We're having dinner. Get that rattletrap off my porch. Yore sorry self, too."

"Yessir, oh, yessir, oh," Mister Swann sang in his slow, sad way, his voice wandering over the words again and again. Then I heard Mister Swann's bicycle chatter across our porch.

Daddy shut the door. He dropped back into his chair. "Well now. Where were we?" he asked cheerfully. Everybody but Gold Ma pretended to be eating. She was looking straight at me, her mean little eyes glowing.

I couldn't bear it. I got up and went to the kitchen.

"Where you goin'?" Daddy called.

"To get a drink of water."

Quick as I could, I fixed up a plate from what wasn't already out on the sideboard. I used Gold Ma's wedding china—with the blue floral design.

"David, whatcha doing?" Daddy was looming beside me.

"Giving Mister Swann Christmas dinner," I said, trembling clear to the core. I expected him to knock the plate from my hand, but I kept on serving.

"Get yourself back to the table—" His hand was a vise on my arm.

But Lucas was suddenly there. He faced Daddy. He was bigger. And burlier. In a burning tone he said, "Maybe *you* better get back there, Franklin. It's Christmas and David has a guest."

All I remember is Daddy swore. And I remember my grandmother's face. Like silence, she'd drifted up alongside us. I knew she longed for Uncle Lucas and Daddy really to be brothers—like they must have been when they were young. I thought, She'll have to wait a damn long time.

Shaking like a sheet in wind, I opened the back door. Mister Swann was waiting quietly outside. He hadn't understood what my daddy'd said, so he'd just gone around back.

"Here, Mister Swann," I said. "It's turkey. With dressing and gravy, cranberries, too. I hope it tastes good."

He took the plate from me carefully. It teetered a little. So did he. He sat down on the steps to eat. I went on in. I looked through the screen at Mister Swann, his hands grubby with rodents and dirt, working delicately at his Christmas dinner as if he were in a fine restaurant.

I watched, immobile, as if I were a statue.

"Old ways don't die so easy, I'm sorry to say." Uncle Lucas sighed. "Ain't nobody holy."

Yeah.

Food had vanished from my mind, presents, too. There on the back porch, before dinner was over, Christmas ended for me.

22.

The year turned. I was still twelve, but about to turn, myself.

As the days passed, certain sounds patterned my life: the crinkle of my daddy's newspaper, the shuffle of Geth scuttling through shrubbery, the sigh of the oven door opening and closing, the clink of dishes being dried after meals, the rat-a-tat of Rain Birds, the clamor of Gold Ma's bell, the smack of bugs against the screens at night, the drone of bone names, shotgun blasts, the yowls of cats.

Thirteen was coming on. At last I'd taken the entrance examination for the Barlow Academy. Daddy'd seen to it that I'd eaten a chunk of chocolate cake before the test—to zing my brain awake. Soon as the school rules allowed, Daddy sent my application in. He'd walked me to the mailbox one day, tapping a long white envelope against his fingers. He'd stuck the letter inside the box, shut the door, and hoisted the little red flag that announced to the mail carrier, *Outgoing mail here.* "Well, sonny boy, it's on its way." Daddy said it like some kind of prayer.

Sometime around then, a light snapped on inside my head. Just like in the funny papers. Pull that little chain, bulb glows bright: I didn't want to go to Barlow. Hell, it was way up North. What would a Southern boy do up there surrounded by Yankees? Fight for four solid years?

I still loved bones and body parts and vocabulary words and all the other stuff I'd been swallowing, but I was sick to death of studying them. And I realized I didn't want to leave home. Or my family. To sever all ties for months on end. Even thinking about it, I could feel a pang of lonesomeness.

It crossed my mind, though, maybe the Ku Klux hadn't made its way there yet, up North maybe there'd be less hate. By now, I was convinced that's why Lucas left us. What crossed my mind most was I didn't want to leave Malcolm. I didn't make a peep about this revelation. Just sat on it like a biddy warming an egg. There was a fly in the ointment, of course: Daddy. ("Sonny boy, you're goin' if I have to drag you by the hair!" he'd say.) In spite of that, I began to consider this new possibility—as if I had a choice.

It was an afternoon in January, and cold. The sky was flocked with clouds gray as geese. The leaves on the oaks were brown and damp from the fog that crept along the ground, a dank live thing. School was still out for the holidays.

For safety, Malcolm and I met an elaborate ways from my house, if we met at all. Though he and I had our future inheritance from Miss Grace to think on, that didn't give us anything much to do right then. We were bored as bed-bugs after the sleepers get up.

"What'll we do?" Malcolm asked, working on a heel of bread dripping with honey.

"Don' know, but let's do it quick." I felt jumpy. Anytime, somebody nursing a hatred could come by and target him. He was a sitting duck.

"I know what," Malcolm said, "let's go over to the graveyard."

"Let's don't," I said right off. The graveyard was creepy. Full of silence. Full of dead people, too.

"You're scairt." It wasn't a question.

"No, I ain't," I said too quick.

"Then let's go."

"Oh, all right. We can make rubbings from headstones, to prove we were there." I suggested that to show I wasn't scared.

"Got paper?" asked Malcolm.

"Shoot, yeah. Crayolas, too." I dashed back and got them from the house, along with two slabs of pecan pie I swiped from the pie closet. Then we took off.

There were no living people in the graveyard but us. Everything seemed peaceful and a little weary. Even the oaks looked tired. The place made me feel like muttering a God-bless somebody.

Malcolm and I wandered among the graves, careful not to tread on one, looking for gravestones to make rubbings. The grass was damp. Soggy leaves clung to our shoes. The silence made us quiet, so we barely spoke. Every now and again I'd catch a whiff of something like death: bunches of rank old flowers drooping over the stones. Some of the markers were just nubs. You couldn't make out the names. As I walked, a sadness seeped into my bones.

"Hey, here's a good one," I said. "'Laura Gentry. Devoted wife and mother.'"

"Ho-hum." Malcolm gave an exaggerated yawn.

"Okay, you find somethin' better."

We poked around. The ground was so hummocky, sometimes I stumbled.

"How 'bout this? 'Our Little Lamb. God took her home to paradise. Age three months.'" On the same stubbed slab was the carving of a simpery lamb.

"Malcolm, that's too sad. I cain't make a rubbing o' that."

By that time the ground fog was thick and creeping over the grass. Clammy tongues lapped around my ankles and gave me the all-overs, but I didn't say so. Evening was coming on, the silence thickening.

"You scairt?" Malcolm asked.

"Hell, no."

"Hey! Looka here!" I read with glee, glad I'd found

it instead of him: "'Dulé Dupree, 1898–1944, Season's Greetings!'"

"What season? I wonder." Malcolm giggled.

I set a sheet of paper over the stone and carefully rubbed it with a Crayola. The paper was soggy and tore. It didn't matter that we couldn't get a rubbing. *Season's Greetings!* was emblazoned forever on our brains.

"I gotta ghost story," Malcolm said after a while.

"Okay, tell it." He could tell the tingliest tales. We settled ourselves against a headstone.

"There was this witchy ghost in a graveyard," Malcolm began in a quavery voice. I giggled some, with fear. "With hair of fog. Its eyes were smoldering coals, and it shone in the dark. That haint rode a behemoth steed, all of bone. And it moaned, *'Woe! Woe! Your darkest hour is nigh—'*"

"Malcolm, hold on," I whispered. "I heard something." It was getting foggier and dark, and sounds took on supernatural qualities.

"You're jus' tryin' to scare me."

"Am *not*. Something's out there."

"You're givin' me the creeps."

"Shush!"

We fell still as the headstones, listening with all our might. Sure enough, somebody—or some *thing*—was shuffling. And it was close. Jesus H. Christ! What if it jumped us? What if it trampled us flat with steed of bone?

"Hear that?"

"*Hell, yes!* The haint with hair of fog!" Malcolm whispered.

"Hush up! It'll hear us!"

Woe! Woe! Your darkest hour is nigh! The chant moaned in my mind.

Suddenly a Presence appeared from behind a tombstone. An eerie illumination. A big creamy moon floating close to the ground. If it beckoned, what would I do? Lord God! Our darkest hour *was* nigh! I nearly jumped out of my skin. I grabbed onto Malcolm and was about to holler "Run!" when the moon grunted.

"Jesus, Geth!"

The sow was rooting through the graveyard, luminous as a revelation. I was never so glad to see a pig in all my life. Malcolm and I flung our arms around her like she was a kissing cousin.

"Geth," Malcolm said, "I just love you to death."

I felt wrung out as a sheet. "Let's get on home," I said.

"Yeah," said Malcolm. "Miss Grace'll be missing Geth." He said it in an offhand way. But for once, he looked scared—like he'd been visited by a ghost.

We walked toward home, blabbing to Geth and urging her along with our sodden rolls of paper. Though the graveyard sounds turned out to be only the sow, I still half-expected a haint to flap up at any moment from behind a tree and strangle me.

Geth's inquisitive snout dragged her hither and yon. There was so much to sniff, she stopped about every two feet at some especially luscious scent. Before us, damp leaves left a dark, slithery swath. We were coming up on the bus stop when Geth started snuffling to beat the band. She hit a trot, making straight for a bench and the figure slumped upon it, sleeping.

"Geth! You come back, hear?"

When we got there, Geth was nosing the man.

"Sorry, mister—" I began. Then I jumped back and stumbled over Malcolm. I wanted to cry out for all I was worth, but only a small animal sound escaped my throat. It was no longer a man, but a corpse.

Though his skin was dark, bruises blued right through it, like ink. His coveralls were darkly stained. He was staring goggle-eyed into the gloom. There was something horrible about his face. I moved closer. God Almighty! A mole had been stuffed down his throat. I stood rooted in horror. Then I threw up.

Slung over the bench where he sprawled, a sign read, COLORED ONLY. Another hung around his neck: ONE LESS NIGGER.

Malcolm and I stared at each other.

At last he whispered, "Mister Swann."

23.

"Mister Swann," I whispered.

"He's dead." Malcolm looked sick.

Mister Swann's traps were scattered; his bicycle was stove in, bent beyond recognizing.

"Where's his cap? Where's his cap?" I kept saying, looking everyplace. As if finding it would put things right.

Eventually I gasped, "What should we do?"

Malcolm snatched the sign from Mister Swann's neck and threw it down. "Don't nobody deserve no tag round him."

I knew better than to touch anything, but I didn't care. I walked up to Mister Swann slowly. Slowly, I put out my hand. Cringing, I tried to yank the mole from his mouth. It wouldn't come. I was sweating and couldn't grip it. So the tail kept slipping through my fingers. It felt so horrid, I puked again.

Then Malcolm and I were sobbing and holding each other for dear life. Suddenly, Malcolm's eyes rolled. "Klan!" he whispered. We looked at each other, terror-struck. Then we ran like hell.

Malcolm tore for Howard. I lit out for home, like a firecracker'd been tied to my behind.

"They killed him! They killed him!" I wailed, busting

into the house. "There was a mole—" My breath heaved in and out as I sobbed the story. "How could they? How could they? How could they?" I kept babbling.

"*Bless Jesus!*" said my grandmother.

She looked bleak with horror, as though her worst fear had come to roost upon her shoulder. Still, she took me in her arms. "There now, David," she said. But she could not comfort me. Nobody could.

Daddy wasn't around. He was tending somebody who'd pitched down his basement stairs and cracked some ribs. My grandmother telephoned Sheriff Roy Hyde. Oddly enough, she was composed as she dialed the number and put the call through. Before long, the sheriff drove up in a squad car, with a deputy.

"Roy, you make this quick," said my grandmother sternly, not a bit herself.

The light was dim and it was gloomy in the room. She sat beside me, one hand over mine, while I told again what I'd seen. I kept trying to make sense of the hateful crime, repeating, "Why? Why?" like a bewildered bird banging against window glass.

The deputy took down my every word. He wrote carefully, as if he were copying a spelling list onto a blackboard. I did my best to speak clearly, the whole time weeping softly. The grown-ups didn't cry. I believe they knew so many terrible things, they were past crying.

Nobody spoke for a time. They sat there and watched me—and each other—knowing.

"Well, thank you, son," Sheriff Roy Hyde said to me at last. "Guess that about wraps it up. 'Night, Miz Church, David."

I knew they wouldn't put much effort into seeking the murderers. It was only the Mole Man. *Only the Mole Man.* That reminded me of something—Christmas. When Mister Swann had come begging. Had Daddy done something worse than refuse an old man dinner? My head swam. Where was he now? I just bet he wasn't setting bones. Suddenly, I was certain that Daddy'd had a hand in it.

When the law had gone, my grandmother said, "Here, David, let me fix you a cup of Ovaltine."

"No thanks, Grandmother, I'm going to bed."

I had no intention of sleeping. I needed to know something, to get at the truth, right down to the very bones. I went straight to my daddy's bedroom. I checked the garments in his closet, fluttering them through my hands. Nothing. I began to rifle the bureau drawers, rummaging for something. A proof—like a hood with eye cutouts. A hood that could hide him while he strangled a Negro.

Every sound made my skin prickle. My blood was drumming in my ears. My legs were turning to water. What if Daddy came in? I'd be dead as Mister Swann.

I opened a drawer, slowly as I could. Even so, it made a low *reeeeench*. To me, a shriek. I was trembling so, the pulls rattled. Then I heard footsteps on the stairs. *Jesus!* Somebody was coming up. My scalp crawled and my heart began slamming against my ribs. "Come on! Come *on!*" I commanded my hands, but they fumbled like wooden things while my brain screamed, *Hide!*

"Whatcha doin', sonny boy?"

The silence that followed was an ax about to drop.

"L-looking for—a handkerchief."

Daddy looked at me real cold. He slammed the drawer shut and uttered a low growl. "Boy, you keep outta my things."

Alone in my room, I sank into sorrow, thinking about Mister Swann. I lay in bed shivering; I couldn't sleep. I had seen many dead things before: lizards, chickens, dogs, bloated heifers with maggots. But till now, I had never seen a dead person, man or woman. Especially not somebody I knew. From some far-off place, I could hear a sad-sweet voice: *What's yo' killin' wants? What's yo' killin' needs?*

Nobody needs killing, I thought. My ghoulish hope for a trip to the morgue was snuffed. I never wanted to see another dead person in my life.

I awoke many times that night. Whenever I did, I heard

a wispy sound. Somebody sweeping, sweeping, sweeping, sweeping.

For a long time after that, I was afraid to go to sleep. Sometimes I still am.

At first there was a flur of talk about the Mole Man's murder. But soon the gossip died down. Our town had swallowed Mister Swann.

24.

I dreamed that it was Sunday. I was seated in church. My family had spread out the entire length of one pew. They sat on either side of me. Gold Ma on my left, Daddy on my right. All around, waxen-faced and soundless as candles, my neighbors were seated. There was a soft muttering amongst the churchgoers. But mostly they were still, being assembled as they were in God's house.

We rose in unison and began to sing a hymn. Our voices mingled. Young, old, creaky, sweet. Then my arms felt oddly light. All at once they lifted like wings. I felt myself rising. Slowly. I floated close to the ceiling of our church. A big lost bird.

Below, I saw all the people I knew. They were wearing their good clothes because it was Sunday. I looked down again. Everything had become white, as if dusted with a sudden blessing of snow. Or draped in yards of angel wings. So beautiful.

Then I noticed that the whiteness was the people themselves—clothed in robes and pointed hoods.

25.

The memory of Mister Swann's murder wouldn't turn me loose. The world had shifted. I felt that I was walking always at a tilt. And every voice seemed somber. Woeful. Slow. A needle dragging over a phonograph record. Like they couldn't quite say what they meant—or maybe it was me. Maybe everybody was fine, but I was hearing the world sad.

"How could he do that?" I asked myself over and over. Daddy was a doctor; doctors don't harm people. After all that time, all that cramming, all those bones, and that longing, I set my mind. Much as I wanted to, I sure as hell wasn't going to be a doctor.

One thing became clear: I had to intercept the Barlow letter. I knew an answer would be coming soon about my acceptance to the academy. Daddy reminded me of that very nearly every day. He was jumping like a flea, itching to hear.

Of course my plan was a loony one. Daddy'd find out soon enough what I'd done. I just hoped he'd wait long enough to inquire to miss the deadline—if I got in. So I began a vigil. Every day I watched till the mail carrier showed up. There was nothing and nothing for a long time. Then it came. My heart lurched when I saw the school emblem on the envelope. Quick as I could, I stuffed the thing into my pocket, then took the rest of the mail inside.

"Mail's here," I told Daddy, calm as a cold-blooded killer. I set the rest of it on the entry table, then I went to my room and I hid the letter.

I wrote Uncle Lucas. He'd up and left the day after Christmas. Nobody'd heard from him since. I wrote anyway. About Mister Swann. About Daddy. I wrote how, though I had no proof, I knew he'd been in on it. I wrote how I feared for Malcolm. I wrote and wrote. And my anger burned the paper.

Uncle Lucas didn't answer. He always answered right off when I sent him a letter, so I knew he was someplace doing import and export.

A fool idea hit me: I decided to visit Tinney. You didn't go down to Howard if you were white, not unless you were looking to put yourself in peril. You especially didn't go if you were a white boy, alone. But at that time, I was stark-raving crazy.

One morning I got up real early. Nobody else was awake. I jumped into my clothes and tiptoed downstairs, stopping only to gobble a cold biscuit. As I went down the front steps, I passed the bottles that the milkman had left. Somebody else *was* up.

Slowly, I eased my Schwinn from the garage. I decided I'd better go there quietly. So one by one, I removed the noisy playing cards from the spokes. Then I slid out our drive.

Though the sky was dark, I could see the first sip of light gathering. And a white rind of moon. Nothing stirred. Even the birds were still sleeping. I was glad I'd removed the cards, though I missed their *whup* as I rode along. Now I was part of the quiet.

Howard lay about three miles from where we lived. On occasion, I'd driven through there with my daddy, who was armed. I didn't much like to go, especially not in our big, fancy car. I felt a multitude of cold eyes on me, mostly from people I couldn't see, but who I knew were there. It wasn't our place, it was theirs.

As I approached, the blacktop petered out to gravel and dirt. So I was forced to go slow. My tires grinding in the gravel made a friendly crunch. While I rode, I thought about Tinney and the questions bottled up within me.

"Knucklehead!" I suddenly said aloud. In my demented state, it hadn't crossed my mind that I'd no idea at all where she lived. Well, I'd just ask somebody, soon as I could. 'Course, they'd know her. Howard wasn't that big.

I rode on, hugging the weeds, smelling their wild perfume whenever I veered from the road and crushed them. Suddenly, the hair at my collar prickled. I turned to look behind me. My tires weren't the only ones spitting gravel. A car had crept up—real close to my bicycle. Slowly, it drew alongside me. A man, a Negro, rolled down the passenger-side window.

"Well looka here what the cat drugged in," he said. "If id idn't."

"Idn't what?" said the driver. He was also a Negro.

"White boy. Color o' grits," said the man, his voice like ground glass.

"Who he look like to you?"

The man peered at me. He leered. "Son of a nigger hater. Le's scuff him up a bit."

The car edged closer to my bike. Fear seeped through me like spilled ink.

"Hey, look out!" I yelled. I was scared spitless. My mouth went cotton dry; my tongue seemed stuck in my throat. I shook so, the bike wobbled.

"You the one better look out, *boy*. Look out, now. Look out," he taunted. The car crept close and closer, the spit of gravel frightening. Then, it nudged my bike, toppling it, and I went sprawling. I heard the car stop. The only sound was the *tick-tick-tick* of the bike wheels still turning. Then feet walking toward me. I felt their shadows before I saw the men. When I looked, the two loomed over me. They were wearing frayed coveralls and shirts the color of faded clouds. Funny how I thought about clouds when I was about to die.

"Git up, white boy," one said, with a foot placed on my shoulder, pinning me so I couldn't. I squirmed and tried to work myself free. The man laughed a dry laugh. He tromped harder. I could smell his sweat, his hatred. Tears stung my eyes. I looked around wildly, trying to see a way of escape. If I bunched up tight, then gave one good wrench, maybe then I could tug loose and—

"Leave the boy be." The words were sharp-edged as a drawn knife. "Git up, son," somebody behind me said. Then he stepped forward, placing himself between me and them.

I scrambled to my feet. I was shaking and crying, smearing the tears on my face with balled fists.

"You stay out o' this, Gideon," warned the truculent one. He spat a glob of venom.

The man, Gideon, was built like a boxcar. His eyes were dangerous. Slowly, he bent down and picked up a bottle from the ground. It was broken, I remember, and green. Gideon gripped it in one huge hand and stood there, legs spraddled, quiet and menacing. "No chance o' that. I'm in it," he said. "Jes' 'cause some white folks behave one way, we ain't gonna act the same. If you think to, I'll show you different. You might oughtta ponder on leavin'."

I believed Gideon could show them plenty. The other men must've believed so, too. Grumbling, they stalked back to their automobile.

"Boy, you say howdy to yo' nigger-hatin' daddy," growled my principal tormentor. "From now on, we'll keep a eye out for ya." Then they spun away in a rooster tail of gravel.

"You all right?" Gideon asked, checking me over. As it turned out, I had a scraped elbow and a skinned knee. You could see how raked up it was through a tear in my pants. "Unh, *unh*," Gideon muttered. "Gotta do somethin' 'bout that. Where you gwine, son?"

"I was looking for Tinney Somebody." I gulped. "I don't know her full name, or where she lives." I was still shaking. And my scrapes had started to sting.

"Yo' in luck. Only one Tinney, here ta Timbuctoo. An' I can make it to her place blinefold."

"You know her?" I said.

"I know her. But I don' know you."

"David. I'm David Church."

"Sorry 'bout this little situation, David Church," said Gideon. "Mebbe if them heathens spent mo' time in such a place as church, they'd spend less time tormentin' boys." His voice was grim. "Come on, now. Get yo' bicycle. Le's pay us a call on Miz Tinney Wilkes."

The house was small and white. Neat as could be. There were so many flowers surging from Mason jars and coffee cans, a sweet fragrance ringed the place. Ring of heaven.

"Prop yo' bicycle up against the porch here," Gideon said. He rapped on the door.

A shadow moved behind a curtain, then the door opened. There stood Tinney, a book in one hand, little glasses pinched onto her nose. She seemed even tougher than I remembered.

"What in the Lord's name—?"

"Oh, jes' a little speck o' trouble," said Gideon. "Th' others got troubled clear away from here. The boy's okay now." He told her about the men.

"I swan! Some folks jes' ain't worth the hide they wrapped in," Tinney steamed. "Lemme lay holda them, I'll crack they heads open like honeydews."

"You take one, I'll take t'other."

"Them two put together got less sense than one roach," Tinney said. "They did, they'd know better'n to mess with white folks. They bes' hightail it."

"Well now. You don' need me for head crackin' at this pa'tic'lar moment, I'll be on my way." Gideon waved and began to walk down the street. Slowly, a small mountain on the move.

"Thank you, Mr. Gideon." I waved at him weakly.

"Anytime, David Church. Anytime."

Tinney bathed my wounds with tepid water. "This'll sting some," she said.

"What is it?"

"BFI. Works so good, they use it in the army."

I gritted my teeth while she tapped the yellow powder from the container onto my scrapes. Tinney was right. It burned like bejeezus.

"So, David," she said, "whad'ya need to tell me that's worth gittin' killed for?" Her face was set, like a stone. She sat me on the sofa, easing herself down beside me.

Suddenly I felt ashamed. There I was down in Howard, with an old dark woman I didn't know, about to spew things I should trust only with Uncle Lucas or Malcolm. I shuddered, thinking about what Daddy'd do if he knew what I was up to.

But I couldn't hold back. My troubles just gushed out about Malcolm and Mister Swann. I think she already knew the whole of it. I talked and talked. The only other sound I remember was the ticking of a clock.

"How can anybody do those things? How can they?"

Finally, Tinney said, "I 'ont know, but Ugly's out there, baby dear. Like a wile animal. You dwell on it too much, you cain't move. You sink into the mud yo' ownself."

"But what about Malcolm?"

"I do my utmost. I watch 'im like a hawk an' I cajole an' I coax an' I bluster an' I threaten—an' I pray. So do all his kin. I could, I'd hogtie 'im to the bed to keep 'im home. He's a willful boy. An' he knows who he wants for a frien'."

"I'm afraid."

"O' what?"

"Daddy's—Klan," I blurted.

So. I'd said it. The dread word slid out and coiled itself in the air.

Tinney stared off somewhere. She mused, "That Franklin, he was the sweetest chile." It was quiet for a time. Then she said, "Klan. Hmmm. Mebbe yes, mebbe no." She added, "Klansmen, ascared as little chil'ren."

I was amazed. They seemed so fearless, so tough. "What're they scared of?"

"Mebbe that coloreds'll take something belongs to them."

"What?"

"Dunno. But seems to me, the one who hates has already lost the most important thing of all."

"What'd he lose?"

"His own human self."

She began to croon. No longer a sibyl, just a mother. Something about "bye-m-bye" and "small pican," mostly words I didn't understand. I felt the hum of it fill me. I believed the song had come from Africa, a long time ago. I believed she'd sung it once to my daddy. Tinney sang, and it was sweet. It lifted a burden from my heart. I understood why Daddy loved her.

❖   ❖   ❖

A rap came at the door.

"Hey, David," Malcolm said, barging in. "Heard you were here."

"I'm here."

He looked at me funny. "You okay?"

"Yeah."

It was still early when Tinney saw me home. For once, Malcolm stayed put. When we reached my house, Tinney remained on the walk. She did not step onto the porch.

Tinney said, "Keep yo' feet out o' the mud."

Then she was gone.

"Where've you been, David?" asked Daddy.

"I don't know. Hanging round. Frittering."

"Frittering! Jesus, boy! Your grandmother's beside herself. I nearly telephoned Roy Hyde to track you down."

"Sorry, " I mumbled, though I wasn't. Not a bit.

"Now you go on in, help with supper."

"Yessir."

So. Daddy was worried about me. But he was angry, too. Good old Daddy. Always swinging between love and hate.

26.

"Where's that letter?"

Before I was fully awake, Daddy was looming over my bed. He was nearly apoplectic.

"I contacted Barlow. They mailed it out way back. I know you took it, and I wanna know why."

"I'm not going, even if I'm in. I don't want to be a doctor anymore."

The room grew real still. Daddy just stared through me for the longest time. I felt cold.

"It's that worthless Malcolm Deeter. Since you've known him, he's had you pissin' away your time. He's not going anywhere with his life, so you don't want to either."

"That's not—"

"Shut your mouth. Give me the letter."

I got up slowly, went to my bookshelf, and pulled off *Gray's Anatomy*. It was heavy. I held it in front of me and cracked it open. The letter slid out.

Daddy pocketed it. He knew what it said.

"I'm not going to Barlow," I said.

"In a pig's ear you're not."

"You can't make me."

"I can. And I will."

27.

On a day in January, I woke up at first light. A single star still held its place in the sky like a single candle. Should be thirteen stars, I thought. I'm thirteen years old today. I wasn't the only person aware of my new age.

"David, you up?" asked Daddy.

He cracked the door and looked in.

"Mornin'," he said, chipper as could be. Like nothing ugly'd happened between us. "The dawn of your fourteenth year. Get yourself dressed. We're going downtown."

Mister Swann had been dead nearly a year. Since then, Malcolm had come around, but like a ghost. He'd scoot in and out, leaving me secret notes in the damnedest places. Whenever I noticed one, I grinned.

My troubles with Daddy weren't forgotten. They'd multiplied. But I remembered what Tinney'd told me: *Keep yo' feet out o' the mud.*

Though I was still boiling, I tried to bury my anger so it wouldn't drag me down.

This day, I decided to go along with Daddy. To pretend we were a normal family.

"Get a move on," he said.

So I took a monkey bath—something I'd learned from

Uncle Lucas. "You jes' th'ow the water up an' run out from under it," he'd told me once, then he'd roared his best belly laugh. I dressed fast, ran a comb through my hair, then thunked downstairs, knowing Daddy'd be waiting on me.

"My stars, David," my grandmother greeted me, "I can't believe you're thirteen." She gave me a little peck on the cheek.

I kept fussing with my cowlick, trying to tame it with spit, till Daddy snapped, "David, for Lord sakes, quit doin' your hair that way. Nobody'll notice on a galloping horse."

Grandmother had fixed a feast to mark the event. Fried ham and sausage patties and a stack of hotcakes swimming in butter, with a little pitcher of warm maple syrup alongside it, and a basket of piping-hot biscuits with honey butter and homemade peach preserves. I was allowed to drink a cup of black coffee to boot.

"Sorry to rush off. Daddy's shovin' me out the door."

We were halfway down the front steps when Daddy said, "You best tell Gold Ma your news before we go, son." Now it seemed like he was always calling me "son." If that made him feel good, let him. I knew his temper'd get the best of him soon. Well, I wasn't going to be like him; I was going to be like Lucas.

"Okay," I said, and let his mood roll where it would.

I slogged upstairs to her room. My fingers were crossed,

of course, to *x*-out that I was there. "Hey, Gold Ma," I said from the doorway. "Today I'm thirteen."

"You're banished!" she hollered, holding fast to old anger. As I retreated, she added, "And you're not worth doo-doodly-squat! *I'm* a hundred!"

Soon I was sitting in the Buick beside Daddy. The top was down. His head was crowned with his fedora. Moth brown, moth soft.

As he drove with his usual lunatic speed, my daddy belted out a chant: *"Rooty toot toot! Rooty toot toot! We are the boys from the institute! We don' smoke an' we don' chew! An' we don' go with the girls who do!"*

For a brief moment, Daddy became Uncle Lucas. Surely, everybody we passed was gawking.

When we reached Main Street, he parked in front of Russ Russell's barbershop. Daddy and his pals gathered there most every day; farmers gathered Saturday nights. Daddy'd once given me this advice: When the farmers come in, you listen good. Then go home and do the opposite.

"Come on, son, we got us bidness to attend to."

"What business?" Daddy only went there for haircuts and shaves. And to chew the fat with his cronies and tell all the lies they could fabricate.

"You'll see."

As we entered, I studied the barber pole that adorned

the outside of Russ Russell's. Like an endless red-white-and-blue candy cane gobbling itself and renewing. How the hell did it do that?

The barbershop was a magical place. Almost nothing'd changed there in a hundred years, Daddy said. It had barber chairs and a counter—a wooden slab—running the length of one wall. The slab held a slew of jars and bottles of all colors and sizes and shapes. There were liniments and unguents and scalp treatments and aromatic products like Wildroot (which I thought Dick Tracy used) and Brylcreem ("A little dab'll do ya"). To one side hung a calendar with a naked woman on it. And a sign: STILL FIGHTIN' THE WAR. In a corner, standing upright in a small glass tank, were black combs drowned in disinfectant. There was special tissue paper to place between a man's neck and shirt collar, and talcum to brush onto that neck when the job was done, and special soap like "the celebrated Kentucky Shaving Soap."

When I was little, Russ Russell'd let me lather up soap in a mug—or even on a customer—for fun. A big ol' horsehide strop hung from the counter nearly to the floor, like a big ol' tongue ready to lick Russ Russell's razor to murderous sharpness, ready to turn a man's chin smooth as stone.

"Mornin', Russ," Daddy said, pumping his hand. Russ Russell was a tall, bony man with a wisp of hair like a kewpie doll's, and expressionless as a hard-boiled egg. Other men of other shapes and sizes occupied the barbershop. Men who knew me like they knew their own children. Millard Bledsoe, the banker, was tipped back in a chair, a snorty snore thundering from his throat.

"Mornin', boys. David's thirteen today."

They all leaned forward and peered at me. "Surely not," Russ Russell said. "Well now. Felicitations, David."

"Thank you, sir."

"Forget the niceties." With bravado, Daddy drew out an envelope, blew into it, then tapped out the contents. I knew what it was and wanted to bolt. "Listen here, you-all." *Hell!* I thought.

Dear David Chambers Church:

With the approach of your thirteenth birthday, it is my distinct pleasure to notify you of your acceptance to the Barlow Academy. A long tradition in educational excellence precedes you, of which you are no doubt aware and which you, as a Barlow scholar, will doubtless uphold. Soon you will receive further information about your academic future. In the meantime, the Barlow Academy extends to you its most heartfelt congratulations.

"It's signed by the damn dean himself." Daddy exulted. He'd puffed up much more, his buttons would've busted and his trousers slid right down. His face was a study. I think he was genuinely proud—and he had me cornered.

The barbershop burst into cheers like a Roman candle. Millard Bledsoe snorted to life. Everybody knew it was a shining moment. Russ Russell seemed especially to know it, but didn't seem quite clear how to mark it. Finally, he asked me, "Wanna shave?"

The Roman candle erupted again—because I had no whiskers.

Russ Russell went to the counter and picked up a bottle from the multitude. He unscrewed the cap, then thrust it at me.

"Have a drink, David."

"Of hair oil?"

Another whoop.

I took a good slug. And I choked. Tarantula juice.

Next, we stopped at Pemberton's Ice Cream Parlor. MILE-HIGH ICE CREAM CONES a sign in the front window blared. Daddy burst through the swinging doors like Wyatt Earp entering a saloon. "Set 'em up!" he boomed. "We got us a birthday boy here!" People swiveled to see who that could be. I was embarrassed but tried to act normal, on account of my daddy seemed to be enjoying himself.

The walls of Pemberton's were papered with oversize pictures of a triple-decker cone, a Black Cow, and other delights. Each time I entered, the fragrance nearly put me in a trance. It was a blend of vanilla, strawberry, chocolate, peppermint stick, pistachio, tutti-frutti—every flavor you could name.

Mr. Broke Pemberton was the proprietor. People said he got that nickname on account of he gave out so many free samples, half the time he was near broke.

"So, tell me, David, how old are you today?" asked Mr. Broke Pemberton.

"Thirteen, sir."

"Well now. If that doesn't call for a Banana Bonanza, I don't know what does. Two Banana Bonanzas comin' up."

"Oh, I don't believe I could eat two."

"You did, you'd explode. The other's for yore daddy."

I flushed so, my hair felt like it was afire.

I sat at the counter alongside Daddy and watched Broke Pemberton assemble our desserts. He took out long glass bowls from under the counter and spurted a little chocolate sauce across the bottoms. Next, he snapped two bananas from a bunch, peeled them, slit them with a knife and set the halves in the chocolate baths. Between the banana slabs he scooped globs of ice cream—strawberry, chocolate, vanilla. He oozed a thick layer of hot fudge over the vanilla blob, strawberry sauce over the chocolate blob, pineapple sauce over the strawberry one. Then he grabbed a can of whipping cream and gave them a good spritzing, till the bowls resembled plowed white fields.

"Nuts?" he asked.

"Yes, please."

"Maraschino?"

"Yes, please, sir," I said. I'd decided to go the whole hog.

So, holding it by the stem, Broke Pemberton plopped a cherry on top of my ice cream.

"Eat up," he said.

We did. I dug in with a long, thin silver spoon and began to devour the ice-cream mountain. After a bit, I felt a raging chill inside my head.

"Ow," I said, rubbing at my temples.

"What's the trouble, son?"

"Something cold's gripped my head."

"You're eating like the train's leaving the station without you," said Daddy. "I expect you've got the brain freeze."

Didn't doctors have a name for every sickness!

When we got home, my grandmother took me aside when she could. She gave me a rolled-up piece of paper with my name on it in code. A butterfly skimmed my heart. I hid the present in my room.

Grandmother Church had fixed a nice supper. Though

I was tight as a tick with ice cream, I somehow made room for a meal—and cake. When supper was over, my grandmother brought the cake to the table. It was ablaze with candles, so many it seemed it might melt on the spot. So I blew them out quickly. My grandmother and Daddy sang "Happy Birthday" to me.

I went upstairs and shut my door. I unrolled the paper my grandmother had handed me and read the blurred words: *Dulé Dupree, 1898–1944, Season's Greetings!* I studied on it a long time. It must have been real hard for Malcolm to go back there for that rubbing.

The last light left the sky. Stars came out to tack up the dark. Except for Daddy's reading the letter, it had been a real good day. I didn't know it then, but the next one would be the worst day of my life.

28.

It was Sunday evening. Daddy had asked some friends over to play canasta. There were two games going at two card tables, four players to a table.

Grandmother Church had prepared her crab dip for the occasion. She'd got the recipe from Miss Grace, and I'd helped her fix it. It called for fresh crabmeat, a bevy of condiments, and—Jude Haggard's idea of a joke—"a pair of Franklin's dirty socks." My grandmother had made a big bowl of the dip, arranged in a nest of chips. I helped her by passing it on request, and also by bringing iced tea or cold drinks or beer or whiskey to the guests. Whenever I got the chance, I sampled the dip.

The front door was open to let the cigar and cigarette smoke out and some fresh air in. The screen door was latched, to keep out bugs. A steady hum of talk and laughter fluttered over the card tables. And the sound of cards being shuffled or laid down.

It was dark outside. The canasta games were going strong when a disturbance began. I looked out the window to see what the fuss was about. A parade of the Ku Klux Klan was crawling up our street. Scores of cars and trucks began to pass by our house. I could hear the motors, some purring, some wheezing like they needed tune-ups.

The interior lights were on in most of the vehicles. And each was full of Klanspeople—men, women, and children— in their robes and hoods. They were moving real slow. I was afraid to look at those people, but I couldn't take my eyes off them. Then I noticed one person in particular—Slur Tucker—clear as day. He didn't wear a Klan costume, just stood to one side in his filthy coveralls, grinning the devil's own grin. "Damn you to hell," I swore, and gave him the finger. He didn't see that, but it made me feel better.

Though it wasn't summer, the air was electric. Like at any moment lightning might strike. I didn't know where they were going, but I knew that someplace, somebody was gonna get hurt. Mister Swann spanged into my mind; fear ran along my backbone.

One of the trucks had a loudspeaker mounted on top of the cab. A whiskey-voice barked over it: *"Nigger! Don't you never fergit yore place! Nigger! Don't you never fergit yore place! Nigger! Don't you never fergit yore place!"*

"Real gallant knights," I said bitterly to nobody.

After the Klavalcade had passed, the players went back to their card games. As if nothing had happened.

"I'll have a Co'-Cola," Miraculous Call said. Furious, I went to the icebox. I was trembling so, the bottles clinked against each other when I got one out. Then I heard the screen door slapping frantically against the latch. Somebody was yelling and pummeling the door. Malcolm. *Jesus!* Like always, he was hereabouts, bucking his luck.

"Slur Tucker, he saw me! He's after me! Lemme in!"

I raced for the door.

"Leave it be, David," Daddy said. He never looked up from his hand of cards.

"Dr. Church, *please*—" Malcolm pleaded.

"Hush up," Daddy said. "Those ol' boys ain't after you. Git on home."

"Daddy!" I screamed. *"Let him in!"*

"He can't ever enter this house," Daddy said flatly. He blamed Malcolm, apart from his dark skin, for my change of heart about doctoring. He was real raw about it.

"The hell with that!"

I opened the door. Malcolm stumbled inside.

A fury seized Daddy.

"Damnation, David! What the hell do you think you're doin'? I told you once. That's all the tellin' you get!" he hollered. The card players went dead quiet. Daddy leaped up and ran down the hall. To the gun rack. Savagely, he snatched up his shotgun. I knew he had plenty of loads. I was filled to the marrow with dread.

Malcolm tore for the porch. I followed.

"No, Daddy!" In slow motion, it seemed, Daddy brought up his weapon.

I ran in front of Malcolm. He gripped me for dear life. "God!" I heard the blast. Felt the jolt. Spun completely around.

I felt my legs melting.

"David!" Grandmother Church rushed to me. Instead of to Daddy. Crazy, how I noticed that—before I slumped to the ground.

"What ha-happened?" I mumbled when I came around, numb and clenching my arm. Somebody was holding a bottle to my nose. Ammonia. The fumes burned my eyes, and I blinked through a sheet of tears, wildly trying to find Malcolm.

I felt sick and dizzy. My left shoulder stung like the devil. My shirt was shredded where the rock salt had struck. Rock salt meant for cats. With my fingernail I dug out a sticky nugget. Though blood was weeping from it, the wound wasn't deep.

So, then. There was nobody killed. For a moment I sat there, stunned. My eyes gauzed over. I felt something shimmering, draining away—a light I would never know again.

I came back to myself. The canasta players were flocked around, clucking like large, strange birds. Down the hall Daddy stood stock-still, holding the shotgun.

"Malcolm?" I said. He crouched beside me, real stiff.

"You all right?" Malcolm asked. His eyes held no light.

"I'm all right."

"Blood brothers. Salt and pepper. Friends forever." Then, Slur Tucker or no, he was gone.

I started upstairs, clutching the banister. I could hear my grandmother calling, "Here now, David, let me help you." Gold Ma's bell was ringing to beat hell.

When I reached my room, I began grabbing things from my chest of drawers. Daddy came in.

"I told you, David. I warned you."

I opened the closet and took down my grip, to pack. My shoulder must have hurt, but I barely felt it.

"I didn't mean to—you got in the way," he said. Like somehow I was to blame. "Here, son, let me see your wound."

I kept on packing.

"Didn't I say I was sorry? Son, what're you doing?" Daddy began to mumble that over and over, suddenly a crazy person.

I never looked up. I stuffed my things into the grip, rough and haphazard. The picture of my mama, my saved-up money from Miss Grace, my clothing. My socks hung out, dark tongues, when I snapped it shut.

"David. *David, don't!"*

Daddy could have grabbed me. Stopped me by force.

But what was the use? He knew he'd lost me; I could tell from his eyes.

I looked at the ceiling where Fats was hanging. With one slash of my bowie, I cut him down. The skeleton man fell clacketing to the floor, bone by bone by bone.

The moon hung over our town.

Already my heart felt lonely as I stepped out into the night. Slowly, I walked down Cherokee Street. Away from my house. I didn't look back. I realized in that moment that I didn't hate Daddy. I just hated a part of him. I was amazed. I had lived with him every day of my life, but I'd never come to understand him. I would always wonder if he'd known before he pulled the trigger that his shotgun was still loaded with salt.

What I would do later, I was uncertain. Tonight, I'd stay at Black Bob Cave. Tomorrow, I'd say my so-longs to Tinney and Malcolm, then head north and find Lucas.

I was a boy named David Church. I was thirteen years old. And I was leaving home.